ALL ROCS WISE & WONDERFUL

THE PORTAL STORMS
BOOK 1

T.M. BAUMGARTNER

1

The zap lizards were at it again.

Two little orange heads peered down at me from their wobbly nest atop the security camera at the side of the veterinary hospital. Between the poor base and a nest building style rivaled only by pigeons, there was a two out of three chance any babies hatched would plummet to the ground before they were old enough to fly. I knew this because this zap lizard pair had tried this same spot three times in the four years since the first portals had opened.

I was not going to interfere. Absolutely not. They were wild animals, not even native to earth, and it was not my problem if they couldn't make better nest building choices. I, Dr. Vanessa Cunningham, was not responsible for every animal on the planet, even if they were ridiculously cute. "Not my circus, not my monkeys," I sang to myself as I rounded the corner. Somehow, the species had survived without me before they had come through the portals — they could figure it out on their own.

Yanking my scarf tighter, I unlocked the back door and slipped inside, pulling it firmly closed behind me. For a moment, I reveled in the peace of the nearly empty building. Everything in the treatment room was orderly and gave off a faint whiff of the bleach used by the overnight cleaners. No fluid pumps beeped, no dogs barked from the wall of cages, and no phones rang.

Within the hour, it would be chaos. Patients would transfer in from the overnight emergency clinic. Other patients that should have been seen earlier would come in crashing. My carefully planned schedule, with slots left open for urgent cases, would be double-booked. I was one of the few doctors in the area who saw xenotics, so it was hard to turn patients away.

But until the phone lines switched over in twenty minutes, I could still pretend.

The coffee in the break room smelled of hazelnut and burnt grounds, but it was either that or nothing at all. I took my mug up to the reception area. Rochelle glanced up, phone headset blinking, and finished writing on a pink message slip before hanging up. Some days I coveted her curly red hair that always seemed one hairpin away from springing into life on its own. But most days I had enough sense to realize my morning routine would leave it looking like I'd stuck my finger in an electrical socket and remained content with my own straight brown hair, chopped off at shoulder length to keep it from tangling.

"Good morning, Dr. C. Did you see the zap lizards nesting on the security camera again?" She bit her cheek to hide her smile.

"Not my problem, dammit."

Rochelle nodded, the grin peeking out. "Nothing too urgent from the weekend." She handed me a stack of message slips and mail. "There's also a consult request for Sac Emergency, but it's from Saturday night."

"About the pigamus? I talked to them." After hours calls from other veterinarians were a constant in my life. I dug through the stack of messages and discarded the request.

Rochelle tapped one perfectly manicured fingernail against the thickest envelope. "They really want you, don't they?"

They were the Chevalier Foundation, a billionaire-funded group with a nebulous mission — something about harnessing the potential of the portals for the benefit of all mankind. It felt like a vanity project to me. Immo Ring, the billionaire in question, was one of those irritating guys who yo-yoed between showy philanthropy and public rage at anyone who didn't show gratitude. If a billionaire really wanted to improve everyone's lives, they could do so without bringing portals into it.

For the last few weeks, they'd been trying to recruit me to a position at a research facility in Maine. As tempting as not having clients might be, I knew it would just be exchanging one headache for another.

Besides, I'd lost my husband when the portals showed up four years ago. I wasn't about to work for an organization that tried to capitalize on them.

"They're barking up the wrong tree. You know I would never leave you guys." I lifted the stack. "Thanks." Pushing open the swinging door into the treatment room with my back, I looked through the messages. As Rochelle had said, nothing was particularly urgent.

Back in the tiny doctors' office, I tore open the envelope from the Chevalier Foundation. *Dear Dr. Cunningham, This week, Chevalier Foundation creator Immo Ring is in talks with the Governor of California to strategize ways to minimize disruption should the state need to be evacuated. We would like to talk to you about a position in the research wing of the foundation, where your work would directly impact the lives of your fellow citizens....* It ended with a handwritten note from Kirk Mullins, the technical director of the research wing, claiming to be excited about working with me and asking me to call him at any time.

The first offer had stressed the salary and relocation benefits, the second had promised I'd be able to hire anyone I wanted, and the third had extolled the virtues of working for a foundation whose goal was to make life better for everyone. Now it appeared we had moved from the carrot to the stick — work for us now or you might get stuck in the chaos if the portal instability worsened.

I sat down, intending to work my way through the pathology reports that had come in since Friday. Then I groaned and stood up again. Stupid zap lizards.

If they couldn't build a safe nest, they really *shouldn't* reproduce. By helping them, I was degrading their gene pool. And yet...

With the step stool in one hand, and a stapler and a flimsy box that had once held syringes in the other, I shouldered my way out the rear door, just in time to see my office manager, Moira, get out of her car.

I held the door open for her as she raised her brows at my supplies. "Not a word."

Everything about her proclaimed her no-nonsense attitude, from her unfashionably bobbed prematurely gray hair to her plain white tennis shoes worn with purple scrubs. "I didn't see a thing." She maneuvered inside with the canvas bags slung over her shoulders. The smell of crushed mint accompanied her.

The instant the door clicked shut, her laughter rang out.

At least my practice co-owner had already taken the work truck out on farm calls and wasn't here to see this. Not that John would miss the results, but if he'd been there, he would have given a running critique of my nest repair job and encouraged the other employees to watch as well.

The step stool crushed what was left of the daffodils. Something had been eating them — possibly native fauna, but I suspected a xenotic. Before the first portals had appeared, nothing had bothered any of the bulbs. Now it looked like I'd have to replace them with something hardier. My mother-in-law swore by rosemary bushes. Maybe I'd try that.

Then again, they were talking about evacuating the entire state. If that happened, I wouldn't have to worry about the afflicted daffodils *or* zap lizard nests.

By the second step, the stool wobbled so much that I kept my balance by gripping the wood siding with my fingertips. "Stupid zap lizards."

The zap lizards in question hissed at me from their terrible nest and a tiny electrical arc jumped from the male's wing to the pole holding the security camera. As defenses went, it was useless against someone my size. I'd been zapped more times than I could count and never felt anything other than a tingle. Likewise with the hissing — their teeth weren't long enough to break my skin, though one had pinched me enough to leave a cute little bruise once.

"Yes, you," I replied, glancing up. They were still too far away. I was going to have to go up to the third step. Hanging on to the wall as much as I could, I shifted up another rung.

One zap lizard launched itself toward my face and I ducked. The step stool dipped sideways. "Oh shit..."

Suddenly, it righted itself and stabilized. "Dr. C!" Moira chided. "Why didn't you wait until I could help?"

I let out a shaky breath. "Yeah. That might have been a

good idea." Now that the step stool had stopped wobbling, it was easier to reach above my head to prod the second inhabitant out of the nest. They would come back after I was done — I'd moved enough nests away from the anesthesia scavenging system outflow to know. Why go to the trouble of building another nest if the first was still around? Which led to another thought... "Remind me to check the roof this week."

"Will do."

This nest comprised three twigs, a plastic drink lid, and a broken fan belt. No eggs yet. I transferred it all to the box and then stapled the box to the wood siding. The staples were meant for paper, but with the added support of the security camera underneath, the improved nest would last until the next high winds. The zap lizards had already returned by the time I climbed down to the ground.

Moira and I admired my handiwork. It looked... Okay, it looked terrible, like a flimsy cardboard box stapled to the side of a building. But at least it was more stable than what had been there before. Maybe the zap lizards had evolved in a place where another species fixed their nests for them. Despite nearly killing myself on the ladder, I felt a sense of satisfaction. Ridiculous.

Rochelle rounded the corner. "Dr. C, animal control called to say they're on their way with a hit-by-car."

Reality always intruded. I lifted and kicked the step stool to collapse it. "Did they happen to say what they were bringing?"

"The dispatcher said a verdiran, but... that can't be right, can it?"

"In this area?" Since the first portals had opened, we'd only met — or recognized — one other sentient species. Verdirans looked almost human, albeit hairless with green skin. They had an embassy on the opposite coast where they retained an air of mystery, rarely leaving the building.

They didn't go out by themselves, and they didn't show up in California. Except I was pretty sure I'd seen one a few weeks ago, during a hike gone wrong. Christopher and I had fled through a portal to another world in order to escape the huge beast hunting us. In the last seconds before we'd returned, I'd thought I'd seen a verdiran. "Call them back and tell them if it is a verdiran, it needs to go to the human hospital."

We definitely weren't set up to treat humans or verdirans. Aside from the legal issues, none of our treatment tables were long enough. Any equipment big enough to use on a human was on the truck with John.

Plus, if it got out that an injured verdiran had been sent to an animal hospital... Even I could see how bad that would look.

I followed Rochelle inside, dumping my nest stabilizing supplies against the wall. While she made calls, I pulled up the XISIS database on the computer, just in case. Surprisingly, there were electrolyte normals listed for verdirans, though it was based on two samples, making it unreliable at best. If I believed the database, LRS ought to be close enough for fluid resuscitation. At least I could pass that along to the human ER.

I heard the back door open and Moira called out, "Dr. C, animal control is here with your hit-by-car."

There was no way they'd be able to fit a verdiran in the animal services truck. I was both relieved and disappointed. It would have been interesting to see another humanoid species up close.

Then I went out back and saw the animal services truck... and an ambulance.

2

Two EMTs stood arguing near the front of the rig. Jeanette Dyer, the animal control officer whom I had last seen on Saturday night drinking margaritas and flirting with the woman tending bar at the Stag, ignored them and opened the back of the ambulance.

"Good morning, Dr. Cunningham."

"Good morning, Officer Dyer." She called me Vanessa or Nessa after hours, but almost always used my title at work, so I did the same. "Your dispatcher claimed you had a verdiran..."

"Happy Monday!" She pulled on the gurney.

"Wait!" I put a hand on the frame to stop her. "They need to go to the human hospital." I looked at the patient. On first glance, one might be forgiven for mistaking him for a bald man, especially with the plaid shirt and board shorts, but the more I looked, the more the differences stood out. His cobbled skin had a green hue, and his features weren't right, though blood and dirt obscured his face. But what I really noticed was the rapid, shallow breathing. "Oh f..., let's get inside. I'll try to stabilize him before transport. Do we know what happened?"

Jeanette helped me roll the gurney through the door Moira held open. "The driver said this guy just appeared out of nowhere in the middle of the road and fell over. The driver *claims* he didn't hit him, but our guy has tire tracks on his leg." She gave a half shrug. "You know how people drive out on the county roads. Drinking coffee with one hand and texting on their phone with the other. This guy was still conscious and moving around when I got there."

I pulled my stethoscope out of my coat pocket, pushed the verdiran's shirt up, and listened in the places I thought his lungs should be. For all I knew, verdirans had just one lung like a snake, and the total absence of breath sounds in the lower left thorax was normal. But a pneumothorax would explain the breathing problems, as free air in the chest cavity collapsed his lung. X-rays would help with the diagnosis, but I didn't think he was stable enough to wait that long.

I reached over to the wall, turned on the oxygen, and handed the attached tube to Jeanette. "Hold this near his nose." Seven fifteen, no technician, and an unstable patient of a species I knew nothing about. What could possibly go wrong? "Moira, can you get some stuff out for me?"

While Moira was gathering supplies, I cut the verdiran's shirt off and cleaned a patch of skin. This wouldn't be a completely sterile procedure, but there was no point in allowing more contamination than necessary.

Resting the side of one hand against the verdiran's ribs, I stretched his skin to keep it from moving and pushed an IV catheter in. The skin was tougher than expected, and the metal stilette bent under the pressure. Just when I was about to stop and nick the skin with a scalpel blade, the catheter went through. I kept pushing until I felt a second pop, which — hopefully — was the pleural wall.

When it came down to it, nearly everything that came through the portals shared common DNA with us. That didn't mean there weren't major differences — convergent and divergent evolution was a bitch — but with nothing else to go on, I had to make a few assumptions. In this case, "do no harm" meant assuming verdirans and humans shared similar anatomy, since doing nothing would leave him gasping for air.

The good news was that it looked like verdirans had the anatomy I'd expected. After I'd sucked half a liter of free air out of his chest, I could finally feel the edge of the re-inflated lung rubbing against the end of the catheter. The verdiran's breathing slowed and deepened. His color went from greenish-grey to a brighter green, which I took as a good sign. When I listened to the lungs again, I heard the expected sounds in all areas, plus a few crackles. I slid the catheter out and tossed it onto the Mayo stand. If the pneumothorax came back, I'd have to consider putting in a chest tube.

Before I started fluids to treat him for shock, I wanted to get baseline bloodwork. I examined his arms, looking for veins. "Okay, Jeanette, now tell me why you brought this guy here."

"Come on, Nessa, you know how bent out of shape they get even thinking about xenos at the human hospitals. They wouldn't have let us past the front doors."

I grabbed her free hand and positioned it to hold off a vein. "Keep pressure there until I say stop."

Jeanette lowered her voice. "And the EMTs told me the ER doctor on duty right now is one of those 'humans first' whack jobs, so I thought things would go better here."

As I pulled blood and distributed it into multiple vials, I thought about that. There was only one human hospital always accessible from here; anywhere else required travel over roads often blocked by portals. Depending on how the ER doctor felt about verdirans, they might refuse to admit this man after stabilizing him, or just refuse to let him into the building at all. As much as I wanted to deny it, this was my circus and my monkeys. "Fine. Where am I supposed to put this guy?"

"I'll call my supervisor and work something out."

While she talked on the phone, I finished cutting the verdiran's clothes off and searched for broken bones or penetrating wounds. The right distal fibula felt unstable, but otherwise, everything seemed intact. So why the pneumothorax? It took me three tries to get an IV catheter in place, which I decided to blame on the tough verdiran skin and not the fact my techs usually placed all my IV catheters.

The back door opened and Laurie rushed in. "Sorry I'm late! Is everyone okay?" She came around the corner and stopped. "Oh. That's why the ambulance was here." She dumped her bag on the counter next to the microscope. "What do you need?"

I handed her the tubes of blood. "Start with these. Then, if you could get set up for rads, we'll start with the chest. I'm looking for anything that might have caused the pneumothorax." A rib broken enough to snag the lung should have been easy to feel, but maybe I'd missed it. I pulled the basket of blood pressure cuffs out and dug through it to find one big enough to fit around his arm.

Rochelle pushed open the door from the reception area. "Dr. C? Couple of quick things?"

"Go ahead." The largest cuff had a picture of a human on it, making me wonder how we'd ended up with it.

"We have a new client walk-in with two spiny rollers that look pretty awful, and she needs to be at work by nine-thirty. Your schedule is full until eleven. Can I go ahead and do it as a drop-off?"

Both the verdiran's pupils constricted when I flashed my penlight into his eyes. "What's my eight-thirty?" If I finished with the verdiran soon, maybe I could squeeze in an extra appointment. While I was thinking, the verdiran pushed my hand away and put his arm over his eyes, a lot like an exhausted person trying to block out light in the middle of the night.

"The Winters dogs. Buckley has a hot spot, and Busy Bee sounds like she has another UTI."

I'd be lucky to get through that appointment by itself without running over. "I guess the rollers will need to be a drop-off then." While I talked, I hooked up fluids to the IV catheter.

"Okay. We also had someone phone to find out if we would see a gravid basilisk. I know you and Dr. Payne said you were still thinking about it at the last staff meeting, so I just wanted to double check."

I looked over at Jeanette. "Close your ears for a minute." Basilisks were illegal to own in California, and the laws on whether we could legally treat them were a bit murky. "Schedule it, but only if the client can follow all the transport rules on the federal website." Rochelle would know which website I was talking about. "Make sure you go over everything on the list before you book the appointment. Anything else?"

"That's it."

"Can you find out if there's someone we should be notifying about this guy here?" The verdirans wouldn't have an embassy nearby, but someone would need to know. That sparked a thought. "Would it be DPAS?"

I knew someone who worked for the Department of Portal Analysis and Security.

"Maybe?" Rochelle scribbled a note. "Either them or maybe the state xenotics board?"

I pulled out my phone and scrolled through the pictures. "I met this guy who works for DPAS a few weeks ago. Christopher Garcia." Even as I continued searching for the picture I'd taken of Christopher's business card, I felt the other three women in the room giving each other significant glances. Any protests I made that it wasn't *that* sort of meeting would be taken as evidence of... something. I wasn't sure how I felt about that, so I ignored them. "Here's his card. If DPAS isn't the right agency to call, he'll probably be able to find out who is."

"Okay." Rochelle wrote his information down. "I'll give him a call and find out." The reception phone was ringing again before the door closed behind her.

Time to reassess my patient. His lungs still sounded normal, the peripheral pulses were stronger, and his heart rate had dropped slightly — all positive signs. Hopefully.

An enormous weight had disappeared when he'd responded to a light shining in his eyes. If he'd had bleeding in his brain, I wasn't equipped to diagnose or treat it. He would either need to go to the human hospital or the veterinary neurologist at the university, which involved traveling up to five hours, depending on the day. Four years ago, it had been a simple ten-mile drive south, but these days, the only safe route involved a long loop through Sacramento, down the Central Valley, and back up through the Bay Area.

Jeanette cleared her throat. "So, this Christopher guy..."

She stopped and cocked her head. "Hang on. Was that the day you bailed on karaoke?"

I frowned at her, pretending my cheeks weren't burning. "Why are you still here?" This was ridiculous. It had been a hike to resupply aid stations, not a date. Even if he had given me his number at the end.

Jeanette laughed. "Ha! I *knew* there was more to that story." She placed a towel on the oxygen tubing to keep it from sliding away. "My supervisor says we've rented the gurney from the ambulance company for the day. I'll leave the paperwork with Rochelle." She grinned and lowered her voice. "And we are definitely talking about this on Saturday."

"Ooh, I think my schedule is filling up. I don't know if I'm going to make it." I ignored her grin. "Go away. I have work to do."

Jeanette laughed again and pushed open the door to the reception area as she pulled papers off her clipboard.

Laurie came out of the x-ray room. "Dr. C, we're good to go for rads. You want a two-view or three-view chest?" She paused. "Lordy, it's a little early in the morning for that." She reached behind her to the stack of towels and draped one over the verdiran's midsection.

"Two is fine. If he's stable, let's also get abdomen and right tib-fib." I boxed an area with my hands to show her the field I was looking for. "Get the left as well, for comparison."

Jeanette came back through, heading for the back door with her radio in one hand. "I have to go. Sounds like it's going to be one of those days."

I waved and pushed the gurney toward the x-ray room. When *wasn't* it one of those days?

3

Forty minutes later, the verdiran was back on the gurney, briefly waking if I bothered him enough. I still wasn't sure what I was supposed to do with him at the end of the day, but it looked like he'd live long enough for that to be a problem.

On the x-rays, I could still see a dark edge of air surrounding the lungs, but that wasn't surprising. As long as no more air leaked, it would fix itself in a few days. I still had no idea what had caused the pneumothorax — none of his ribs were broken. Blunt force could cause a lung to rupture, but I didn't see any bruising. Not that it mattered as long as it all cleared up, but it was weird.

Laurie added a line to the inpatient whiteboard. "What do you want to put for his name? Calling him 'Animal Control Stray' feels a little..."

I winced. "Yeah. Call him... Fred." We would update the board when we found out his real name.

"Fred it is." She finished writing and capped the pen. "I'll tape a cage card on the bed."

The fibula fracture looked like a prime candidate for a

cast. If it didn't heal, we could deal with it later, but I wasn't about to rush into orthopedic surgery. We had no information about how verdirans handled anesthesia, and this verdiran already had a compromised respiratory system.

By the time I'd smoothed the last of the fiberglass cast into place, the receptionists were hovering to remind me my first two appointments were waiting in rooms and there was yet another walk-in out in reception. On her second trip to the treatment room, Rochelle added, "I've left two messages for your friend Christopher, but haven't heard back yet. Do you want me to call the main DPAS number or hold off?"

"Let's wait a bit." The verdiran was stable. Christopher had said he was the only DPAS employee in the region. For all I knew, he was busy tracking another goliath this morning. "If he hasn't called back by lunch, try the main office."

"Will do. I'll go let the walk-in know it might be a while." She read the whiteboard. "His name is Fred?"

"It's a placeholder."

Rochelle nodded, sending corkscrew curls bouncing. "I'll update the computer."

This would not be the morning I made it through Saturday's pathology reports.

Pulling on a clean lab coat, I went over patient orders with Laurie, then left her to monitor the verdiran and restore some order to the treatment room.

On the first chart, Rochelle had written the presenting complaint as "pt licking her hoo-haw x 2 days." Forcing a smile, I opened the door. "Hello, Mrs. Winters. Sorry about the delay — we had an emergency this morning. So, what's going on with Busy Bee and Buckley today?"

                              ∿

By the time the noon appointment break rolled around, I had hospitalized two dogs, a cat, and a musk slinky for treatment. I hadn't even looked at the two spiny rollers dropped off earlier, and I had fourteen calls to return. I would have been even further behind, but my first client was a portal researcher, and she'd been so eager to get out in the field to take more readings that she had skipped describing every symptom of her dog's recurrent urinary tract infection. According to her breathless explanation, the numbers at the portal data collection stations had gone off the charts during the night.

The verdiran's vitals had remained stable, so we'd pushed his gurney to the side of the room and everyone worked around it. Laurie and the other morning technician, Kathleen, wrangled a cat who hissed his displeasure at the blob of ultrasound gel I'd just put on his shaved belly. His periodic efforts to sink his teeth into my hand had a certain rhythm, giving me a chance to look at his organs in between.

As I was giving the cat a break before taking a second look at his liver, John walked in, covered in drying mud from head to toe. Amid the chorus of hellos, he looked around and grinned. "Rochelle said you were having a busy morning. She wasn't kidding." He raised one mud-encrusted eyebrow at the sleeping verdiran. "I'm surprised they didn't take him to Memorial. Let me get cleaned up and you can fill me in." He pulled his duffel bag out of the doctors' office, and paused, reaching over to grab the Chevalier Foundation envelope from my desk. "They're upping their offer again?"

I shrugged. "More of the same."

John dropped the envelope back on my desk, switched the treatment room speaker to his Louis Armstrong playlist, turned up the volume, and headed back to the indoor dog runs as he sang along.

Either the cat in front of me was a fan of jazz, or the drugs I'd given to mellow him out finally kicked in; he stopped squirming long enough for me to get a good look at his liver, which was brighter than it should have been but looked otherwise normal. "You, sir, are getting a feeding tube, and then it's home again." I wiped the excess goo off his belly and Kathleen let him rest in a cage where he crouched behind the cardboard box we'd given him for shelter. I updated his line on the treatment board.

The hospital didn't have a dedicated shower, but the faucet in the dog runs was hooked up to the hot water. As long as you didn't mind getting naked in an empty chain link dog run and holding the sprayer over your head, you could get reasonably clean. In ten minutes, John was back, dressed in a clean set of scrubs featuring ice-skating penguins. "Where we at, boss?"

The "boss" was his way of reminding me I owned 51 percent of the hospital to his 49. He usually brought it up when there was a big decision to be made, or, like now, when he wanted to help out without taking over. Our relationship could have been tricky — he was older, he'd been the sole owner of the practice for decades, and I'd worked for him before I'd graduated from vet school. We easily could have slid into our old roles. That we could work this well together now was mainly due to his insistence that I was in charge.

I quickly rounded with him on the hospitalized patients, including the verdiran, and we went over the items on the treatment board, deciding how to split things up. "You want dibs on anything?"

"How about we send Laurie on her lunch break now, and I'll have Kathleen help me put the feeding tube in the cat, while you and Moira look at the rollers." He added tech and doctor initials next to the procedures on the whiteboard as he worked his way down, automatically keeping track of staff breaks and approximate procedure times. "Do you have a plan for what we're doing with your big friend over there?" He glanced at the whiteboard. "Fred?"

"We had to call him *something*." I looked at the verdiran, who'd been sleeping in the noisy treatment room for nearly four hours. Anyone who could manage that had to be exhausted. Maybe he really *had* fallen down before the car hit him. "I have a... contact in DPAS who isn't answering his phone."

John would have caught that pause as I figured out how to refer to Christopher, so I kept going, hoping to distract him. "I assume they'd spring for a hotel room or something, but he's going to need to be monitored overnight, no matter what. There's no bruising on his chest — I'm not convinced his pneumo was caused by the car." Without knowing what had caused the pneumothorax, I couldn't be certain it wouldn't worsen again. "He *should* be over at Memorial, but..."

John and I shared an expression that was part eye roll, part shrug. Over the past four years, I'd learned not to underestimate phobias, especially about anything outside this planet. The human hospital would have the staff and space to care for a verdiran, but Fred might be better off in the middle of my chaotic treatment room.

Rochelle pushed open the door and leaned in. "Dr. C, your DPAS friend, Christopher, called back. He'll figure out who to notify about Fred, and he'll be here in a couple hours." She let the door swing closed again.

I lifted both palms with a flourish. "Tada! Problem solved."

4

Spiny rollers looked a little like a cross between a large hedgehog and a small ferret. At least, they were supposed to. They had been pretty rare until a few months prior when they had exploded onto the pet market, so we hadn't seen many of them at the practice. I would have been happy to see even fewer — too many people rushed into buying one without researching their housing requirements.

These two looked like the "before" side of a dandruff shampoo commercial. Patches of flakey skin showed through where spines had fallen off. Instead of bouncing around inquisitively as healthy rollers would do in a new place, they were curled up in the corner together, occasionally rousing to scratch at themselves.

Moira pulled on thick leather gloves. Roller spines were sharp enough to pierce skin when they bristled, and they sometimes bit when restrained. "You ready, Dr. C?" She pulled the first one out of the carrier and kept her hands near him on the exam table, leaning on her elbows as she looked at me. "So, where'd you meet this guy from DPAS?"

Sighing, I did a quick exam of the whole animal. I'd known questions were coming. We spent too much time crammed together — nobody had any secrets. "He went along with me on a hike to resupply the aid stations. Why is everyone making such a big deal of this?"

"I don't know." She repositioned the roller so I could pull blood from his back leg. "Something about you seems different lately." She taped a cotton ball over the puncture I'd made while I transferred blood into tubes before it clotted. "Everyone wants you to be happy." Moira swung the roller around so I could scrape the edge of one of his bald spots.

"It's not like that. We were hiking, he dislocated his shoulder, and I got it back into place." We'd also run from a goliath, gone through two different portals, and saved each other's life multiple times. He'd given me his number... and I hadn't called. "We're just friends." I scraped the scalpel blade off in oil on two slides. "Next one."

Moira swapped rollers. "Maybe you should invite him on another hike. Or dinner. Rochelle says he sounds nice."

We definitely wouldn't be hiking on the same trail we'd taken before. The area had become unstable, with portals popping up all over and dangerous animals roaming the hills. "When would I ever have time?" This roller looked about the same as the other, with the added problem of splitting toenails.

"There's that." Moira manipulated the roller so I could pull blood and get another skin scraping, then put her back in the carrier. She spoke to the animals, who were now curled in the back corner. "What do you guys think about some nice meal worms and greens? I bet you'd enjoy that, wouldn't you?" She went off to set up an incubator for them while I looked at the skin scrapings under the microscope. As I'd suspected, they were loaded with mites. While the translucent creatures squirmed on the slide, I took a picture and attached it to the records. Treatment for the mites would be simple, but the owner needed to fix the husbandry issues or the parasites would take over again.

Fred woke up while I was on the phone with the owner of the rollers. I watched him take in his surroundings as I talked about what I'd found. While I commiserated about how expensive meal worms were and gently stressed cat food wasn't an appropriate substitute, he stared at the numbers flashing on the fluid pump. "I'll print out some information and we can go over it when you come back to pick them up this evening." When I looked up after logging the client communication, Fred's eyes were closed again.

Jeanette came through the back door as I was suturing the final laceration on a German Shorthair Pointer. In one hand, she held a trap with three little squeaking bundles of fur, and in the other a takeout bag from BB's Barbecue balanced on a box of two dozen cookies. She cleared a space on the counter by pushing a leash and glucometer off to the side. "I won't bother asking if you've had lunch yet."

The tantalizing smell of grease and spice filled the room as I tied off the suture. "Is that a bribe? Do I want to know what's in the cage?"

"I'm hoping you can tell me what they are and what to do with them. And I'm not allowed to offer bribes. We have rules about that. This is a non-binding thank you in advance."

"To-may-to, to-mah-to." Since half of Jeanette's job comprised picking up the weird animals coming through portals, she was great at identifying xenotics. If we were getting creatures she'd never seen before, it was just more proof the portals were changing.

Kathleen and I lifted the sedated dog down from the

table and got him settled on a blanket in a cage. "Once he's sober enough to walk better, go ahead and call mom. Same meds and discharge instructions as the last time." I scratched the dog's ear. "Stay away from the barbed wire, okay?"

The barbecue sandwich tasted heavenly. It technically didn't qualify as *healthy*, but it was better than the alternative, which was the See's candy stashed in the break room freezer. None of the local restaurants delivered at lunchtime, and I'd run out of frozen food.

Jeanette wandered over and read the card taped to the gurney. "His name is Fred?"

"I doubt it. But it's bad enough he didn't go to Memorial. Can you imagine what would happen if we forwarded his medical record and it said 'Animal Control Stray'?"

Jeanette grimaced. "Crap. I didn't even think about that." She wandered back. "Does this violate the rule about not naming things?"

The rule she referred to was *Never name the wildlife.* "Fred's not wildlife." Giving wildlife a name was a big step in forming an emotional attachment. That was a dangerous road to travel down. I didn't plan to get emotionally attached to Fred, either, but I'd at least treat him as a person.

As I ate, I peered into the trap. The things inside looked a bit like week-old kittens, but with longer bodies and elongated heads. Either they were something I hadn't run across before, or the babies looked different enough from the adults that I wasn't making the connection. I wouldn't be giving these guys names. "No clue. Where'd you find them?"

"A couple miles north of town, where 99 dead-ends. But someone's cat brought them home, so I have no idea where they started out. The cat's owner was going to keep them,

but they scratched the bejeezus out of her arm, so she
called us."

Four years of constant warnings not to interact with
unknown xenotics, and people still couldn't resist the urge
to take them in as pets. I now understood how there could
be people who still drove without seat belts.

All my techs were on their lunch break or already busy,
so I crammed another bite of barbecue in my mouth, then
put a fresh towel on the treatment table and got out the
gram scale. "Let's do this." I pulled on leather gloves and
scooped up the one with grey fur.

The moment I lifted it, the bundle of fluff grabbed the
glove with its mouth and made strong digging motions with
its front legs, revealing razor sharp mole-like claws. The
glove protected my hand, but I could see the lines left in the
leather. "If these things grow much bigger than this, we may
be in trouble." I set it down on the scale and gently pulled
my hand away. "One hundred and two grams." While
Jeanette wrote that down, I picked up the little creature
again, this time by the scruff. It went limp until I set it down
on the towel, at which point it started squeaking again.

Jeanette took a few pictures with the practice's camera
while I quickly examined the baby. Whatever it was, it had
sharp little teeth poking through the gums, so I was betting
it was some sort of carnivore. When I had finished examining all three, I gave each one subcutaneous fluids. Most
babies could go a short time without food, but dehydration
killed quickly.

Once they were back in the carrier, I posted the pictures
on the veterinarian-only xenotics webpage in hopes that
someone else knew what they were, and picked up my sandwich again. "If I can't find any info, I'd recommend starting

with diluted KMR, but honestly, if we can't identify them, their chances aren't good."

Jeanette shrugged. "They're cute little rugrats, but I'm not even sure they're something we want to keep alive. Is there any way they can stay here for the day? We're having staffing issues at the shelter..." She trailed off and stared at the box of cookies.

Saying the county shelter had staffing issues was like saying water was wet. They'd lost a few key people during the initial portal storms, and the temporary director had alienated almost everyone else, leading to rapid turnover in jobs that were already hard to fill.

"You're going to owe me lunch for a week at this rate."

"Thanks. I have the paperwork in my truck."

By the time Jeanette was back, I'd set up a cage with a heating pad on one side and a bright orange caution sticker on the cage card with "Will scratch!" in big letters. I transferred the babies into the cage and then clipped the leather gloves I'd used to the front.

Jeanette handed me a stack of papers. "That should be everything for these guys." She set a leather satchel down on the counter. "This was at the scene with the verdiran this morning. I didn't find any ID, but I'm pretty sure it belongs to the... Fred."

"Did you see anything that might be a phone number?"

"No. There's a notebook with some drawings and writing I couldn't read and some newspaper clippings. But no phone and nothing that screamed 'In case of emergency, contact', at least, not as far as I could tell. He's still not conscious?"

"He's sleeping." I frowned at the verdiran as I considered. "It's possible the driver was telling the truth about him falling over before he was hit." Something about the causes of a pneumothorax knocked against my brain.

Jeanette's radio beeped. "I've got to get going. I'll be back around six to pick up the babies unless you tell me otherwise." She grabbed the empty cage and headed out the back door.

In the doctors' office, I balanced the second volume of the veterinary internal medicine textbook on top of a pile of other reference books. Most of the pneumothorax entry discussed traumatic causes, secondary to being hit by a car or kicked by a horse. Lung disease was another cause, but I hadn't seen anything on the x-rays that would back that up. Occasionally, there was just a weak part of the lung leading to a spontaneous leak of air into the chest. Not what I was looking for. I closed the book and shoved it back on the shelf.

My internet search gave me the answer I'd been looking for. Spontaneous pneumothorax was associated with a history of scuba diving or high altitudes. Not many dogs went scuba diving or flew planes, which was probably why the veterinary textbook hadn't mentioned it.

The verdirans didn't seem to have advanced technology. They certainly hadn't been seen with scuba equipment or airplanes... but I *had* seen a verdiran when I'd gone through a portal to an icy mountainside, and the air had felt thinner there.

Was this the same verdiran? Even if he wasn't, I suspected he'd been traveling through portals. If he was doing that on this coast, where portals might appear or collapse at any second, he was either desperate or he knew how to navigate them.

I thought about that as I went back to the treatment room to write orders for the sharp-clawed babies. If we could learn how to navigate the portals, we could make it safer to stay here. Maybe we could even track down people who had disappeared.

I was still thinking about that when Moira came back to tell me my next appointment was ready.

5

I was carrying a forty-pound pigamus with a lump above its eye when I saw John and the verdiran making their way down the back hall. Fred was now wearing a pair of blue scrubs, with one leg slit up the side to accommodate the cast. John was supporting most of the verdiran's weight.

"You're awake." I smiled and held the treatment room door open for them and then handed the pigamus to Laurie. Looking like a cross between a pig with tusks and a hippopotamus with horse's hooves, pigamuses were about the size of obese border collies. They usually were reasonably friendly, especially if you had food, but they were strong and they could kick with their hind legs, which most people didn't expect. Even knowing they kicked, I still ended up with bruised shins on a regular basis. "Is there anyone we can call for you?" Did verdirans use cell phones?

Fred looked at me blankly.

John shook his head. "I don't think he understands English. But you'll be glad to know the concept of indoor plumbing is familiar." He helped Fred back onto the gurney, reconnected the IV line, and restarted the fluid pump.

"Maybe Christopher — the DPAS guy — can contact a translator. He should be here soon." I got slides and syringes out of the drawer. "Ever seen a pigamus abscess like this?"

He leaned over to look, then poked at the fluctuant lump. "I saw one with a toe abscess, but it was more caseous." He smiled at the slides I had out. "I'd aspirate it."

Steadying my hand on the pigamus's head, I popped the needle into the lump and pulled back a few times on the syringe. No fluid came back, but hopefully I'd gotten enough cells in the needle to get a diagnosis. After I blew the contents onto a slide, I held the glass up to the light to see if anything was on it.

Laurie yelped and jumped back. My hand shot out to keep Julius the pigamus from jumping off the table before I saw what had startled her. A mass of small pale worms wriggled out of the lump.

John picked up a worm. "There you go. Not an abscess." He turned it back and forth. "Looks a bit like a rice noodle, doesn't it?" He grabbed a specimen jar from the cupboard above the microscope and dropped it inside. "Anyone else feel like Thai food tonight?"

I took the jar from him and added the other worms, flushing the pigamus's wound with saline to make sure I got them all out. When I was finished, I held up the jar. The worms weren't anything I recognized. A friend from vet school worked as a parasitologist for the state — she always liked it when I sent her weird stuff. Then, just to prove to John that he couldn't gross me out, I added, "Now I'm craving garlic fried noodles."

Behind me, Rochelle cleared her throat. "Dr. C, Ranger Garcia is here from DPAS."

I closed my eyes briefly and then put the jar down on the counter where it wouldn't get knocked over. When I turned, Christopher stood next to Rochelle, trying to smother a grin. Time to pretend I hadn't said anything. I suddenly didn't know what to do with my hands, so I shoved them into my lab coat pockets. "How's the shoulder?"

He was taller than I remembered, his black hair freshly trimmed, wearing a tan buttoned shirt with the DPAS logo embroidered on the chest. Without sunglasses hiding his eyes, he seemed more approachable. Or maybe it just felt that way because we'd spent so much time together. "Better. I start physical therapy next week. My doctor said I should thank you for getting it back in the socket so quickly. How's the gremlin?"

"Almost all healed up." The blue-wing gremlin we'd rescued during our hike currently lived at my house, though my mother-in-law, Antonia, took Taco along on outings so the tiny creature didn't get lonely.

It occurred to me there were a lot of people standing around, not a common state in the busy practice. "Thanks for bringing him back, Rochelle. Laurie, can you take Julius back up to mom in room two and let her know what happened? I'll try to get these identified and see if there's anything else to add, but in the meantime, have her keep an eye on it and call if it looks like the bump isn't healing nicely."

Ten seconds later, only John remained. Since I couldn't send him away, I had to introduce him. "Christopher, this is my practice co-owner, John." While they were greeting each other, I glared at the two receptionists who had come back to stare through the treatment door window. They grinned and disappeared.

"And *this* is the reason I called you." I nodded toward

Fred, who was watching us. Then I internally cringed. Had that sounded like I was making the point that I'd called him for non-date reasons? Christopher had given me his number after the hike, in case I ever wanted to have coffee. He'd probably heard that as a flat-out rejection. Not that I had decided what I wanted to do, but...

Unaware of my mental hamster wheel, Christopher smiled. "I'm glad you did." He gave a quick bow to the verdiran, then turned to me. "How is he doing?"

Giving medical information let me relax. "Better now. He had a collapsed lung, but I haven't needed to pull air from his chest again, so I think he'll be okay. The leg should heal without surgery as long as he keeps off it." And as long as verdirans healed as well as humans did, which I didn't actually know.

"Good." He turned back to the verdiran, froze, then looked at me over his shoulder. "Why does that say his name is Fred?"

I met his eyes. "Because it sounds better than 'Stray brought in by Animal Services'. That would be the default."

He took a careful breath. "Okay. I've been told formality is very important to them, but you're right. You had to call him something."

I employed my I'll-try-to-help-in-any-way-I-can voice. "We can change it to 'Sir Fred' if that will help."

Christopher ducked his head, hiding a smile. "If I send you a picture, can you print it out?" When I nodded, he pulled his phone out and started tapping on it. "There's a translation app that I'm trying to get authorization for, but in the meantime, I had a friend of mine screenshot something that says who I am and that I'm here to help him." His phone whooshed and he looked up. "As long as he reads the same language..." He shrugged. "So far, every verdiran we've met has used a common language, but that may just be a sampling artifact."

The picture had multiple columns of intricate glyphs. I sent it to the printer in the reception area and then went up front to retrieve it. Aside from a few raised eyebrows, everything had gone back to normal.

Moira waved from the other end of the hall as she closed the door to room three. "Dr. C, I have your next one ready."

I glanced at the wall clock. "Aren't you supposed to be gone already?"

She gave me a sly grin. "I'm going now. Just didn't want to leave too early."

Great. My whole office had been waiting to see Christopher. Not that I knew how I felt about him. Sure, he seemed reasonably nice, and he didn't hold it against me that I'd been the one to force us to keep going when we should have turned back. And he'd given me his number in case I was interested. But still... I was married. Sort of. Maybe. I wasn't sure I was ready to be single and looking again. There were advantages to being alone.

When I gave the paper to Christopher, he handed it to the verdiran, who squinted at it with his head cocked. It made me wonder how accurate the translation was.

"Now what?"

Christopher tapped on his phone. "Now I keep sending texts until I convince someone to let me have the translation app." He looked up and smiled. "I can be really annoying when I put my mind to it."

That I already knew. "Make yourself comfortable. There's some horrible coffee in the break area." I gestured toward the short hall in the back corner. "I have to go see patients, unless you need something."

He sat down on the stool in front of the microscope. "No, no, go on and do your IRS accountant thing. I'm fine."

My cheeks flushed. Trust him to bring up the lie I'd used to keep people from asking too many questions about my job. Halfway through our hike, he'd called me on it. I had the feeling I'd never live it down.

BY SIX O'CLOCK, I'd seen all my appointments and discharged everything that was going home — except the rollers, whose owner wasn't answering the phone. She'd told me she'd be there two hours earlier, so either she was running really late, or she wasn't coming at all. Pet abandonment didn't happen frequently, but it occurred often enough that I'd made a rule banning drop-off appointments for new clients. And then, like an idiot, I'd ignored my own rule. I only had myself to blame. "Go ahead and set the rollers up for the evening," I told Joey, my afternoon tech, when she asked.

Christopher and Fred were over in the corner, mostly out of the way. I'd thought the authorization to use the translation app had come through, because they were both peering at his phone. Then I caught a glimpse of the screen and realized they were watching a soccer highlights reel with the sound off.

I still hadn't identified the fuzzy babies, though one vet in New Jersey said they looked similar to a roadkill carcass she'd seen once. Joey had attempted to feed them milk replacer throughout the afternoon, with mixed results. They wouldn't suckle from a nipple, but with enough time they would swallow the liquid dribbled into their mouths. There was no way the shelter staff could feed them unless we found some way to speed up the process. I didn't have high hopes for their survival.

I got out the smallest one and syringed KMR into it every time it opened its mouth to squeak. A hissing noise behind me had me turning, even before Christopher said, "Nessa? I think there's something wrong."

When I looked over, Fred was sitting up and pulling the blanket off. I took a step toward him. "Wait, hang on. Don't you dare stand on that leg." I put the little creature back in the cage.

By the time I'd turned back, Fred had pulled out his IV catheter.

"Dang it, I was proud of that thing." No, he probably didn't need it anymore, but still. I grabbed a pad of paper and a pen from the counter, remembered we still had his satchel, and grabbed that as well.

When I handed over his satchel, he dug around a bit, slipped a chunk of carved wood into the pocket on his scrub top, and pulled out something that looked like beef jerky and put it in his mouth. He examined the pen for a moment. I took it back, uncapped it, and scribbled a few circles on the paper before handing it over again.

While the verdiran drew on the paper, I turned off the fluid pump and threw out my beautifully placed IV catheter. After a few lines, Fred turned the page around. Christopher and I crowded together to get a better look.

It figured. Four years of undergraduate college, four years of vet school, six years of clinical experience, and what I really needed was the ability to play Pictionary. "Either his drawing skills are as bad as mine and that's a cow, or he can draw and I've just never seen whatever it's supposed to be."

Christopher turned his head sideways. "No, I think that's

supposed to be a cow. That's a horn, right?" He pointed to a triangle I'd thought was an ear.

"Ugh. Hang on." We both had phones with us, but if we needed to look at the same screen, I wanted something bigger. I scooted into my office, slipped past John, and grabbed my tablet.

"Oh, hey, we're on the move," Christopher said.

When I turned around, Fred was already out of bed and standing next to the cage of the unknown babies.

"Wait, wait, wait!" Picturing his arm shredded by those cute little balls of fluff, I sprinted across the room as Fred took a strip of meat out of his mouth and placed it in the cage. Then I skidded to a stop as he picked one up by the scruff and placed it atop the meat. The squeaking stopped. I looked inside and saw all three babies latched onto the partially chewed morsel, digging at it with their front claws, and nosing out and swallowing the tiny pieces that came off.

Fred closed the cage door carefully, then limped back to his bed.

I regarded him. He *knew* things.

"That's a laugh, by the way."

I blinked and looked at Christopher. "What?"

He nodded toward the verdiran. "That thing he's doing with his forehead, the way it wrinkles? That's what they do when they see something they find funny." He shrugged. "It was in one of the documents they sent me this afternoon. To minimize interspecies misunderstanding or something."

"Well, I'm glad he finds my worry about his safety entertaining," I grumbled. "Do you think we can get more specifics about what those babies will eat?" It took a moment, but I brought up a picture of raw steak on the tablet. "This?"

Fred looked at the tablet and made a smoothing gesture

with his hands. I stared at him. He repeated the gesture. Christopher shrugged when I checked with him.

I looked toward the office. "Hey, John, you're better at miming than I am. Come help us."

The chair squeaked, and John ambled out. He did a double-take when he saw the babies eating. "You figured out what to feed them."

"Not me. Fred." I showed him the drawing. "But there's no way jerky has enough calcium for something that young."

"Try a picture of ribs. Maybe they gnaw on bones." John took the tablet and brought up a picture of uncooked beef spare ribs. That got us the same smoothing gesture.

The three of us looked at each other. John shook his head. "Really calm beef?"

"Thanks," I said. "That's super helpful."

Christopher took the tablet. "Maybe dried out, like what a scavenger would eat?" His first search made him wince, but he eventually found a photo of roadkill. The verdiran tapped the screen edge twice with the tips of all five fingers, pulling his head back when that made the picture change. "That's a yes," Christopher said. He mimicked the motion, tapping his fingertips on the edge of the gurney. "That was in the document, too."

I raised an eyebrow. "Any way we can get a copy of that document?"

He shook his head. "They're keeping all the info about verdirans locked down. I'm not supposed to share anything with anybody. Sending it to you would leave a digital trail, and I'm not ready to get fired yet." Then he tapped on his phone and passed it to me. "But if you read it on here, they won't know."

The file was only a few screens long and looked like it

summarized a much longer source. While individual verdi-rans had food preferences, nothing served to them had caused problems. Alcohol seemed to have about the same effect as it would for a human of similar size. "Good to know we're not likely to accidentally poison him."

John blew out a breath. "As long as you're not cooking, anyhow." He laughed when I elbowed him.

The next section had common expressions, with blurry images that looked like they were taken from a video. Wrinkling the forehead meant they found something humorous, moving the lower jaw forward suggested disagreement, and their level of agitation could be determined by how often they blinked. Tapping with fingertips meant yes; slapping the palm down meant no.

After that, it stressed the importance of propriety. Infractions led to various levels of social rejection, all the way up to permanent shunning by all verdirans. A footnote claimed suicide was the usual sequel, though that hadn't been confirmed.

The last section claimed all verdirans carried a chunk of wood with them they were unwilling to be parted from, and speculated about possible religious significance.

I really wanted to read whatever this had been summarized from, but if they weren't letting people outside of DPAS read the summary, I doubted I'd get the original.

John stopped squinting at the phone and turned to me. "So, do we have a plan for the night?"

With Fred's lung injury, he couldn't be left alone overnight. John lived in a second-story apartment without an elevator, and Christopher — who could arguably have been responsible for Fred — lived in a trailer behind the burned-out shell of the house he'd just purchased. That left a hotel or my house, and I preferred to spend the night in comfortable surroundings. "My house? It's either that, or I stay here to keep an eye on him."

John nodded. "I'll let the emergency clinic know I'm on call tonight." When I opened my mouth to protest, he raised his eyebrows. "Even you have to admit, you can't be in two places at once."

"Fine, but call me if you need me." The after-hours emergency clinic treated dogs, cats, and other small pets, but none of the staff veterinarians were comfortable with xenotics. That left one of us — usually me, since I was the one who saw most of the xenotics and did 90% of the practice surgeries — on call nights and weekends.

John dragged his finger in a cross over his heart. Then he glanced at his watch. "If I buy spare ribs on the way home, I can pop them in the dehydrator tonight and bring them in tomorrow."

"Thanks."

Christopher's phone rang, and he moved away to take it. From what I could overhear, he'd finally been granted access to the translation app, and whoever was on the line was walking him through the installation.

That was good. I had questions for this verdiran.

When John went back to the office, I did some calculations. It would be beneficial for the baby whatsits if we kept them here instead of sending them off to animal services. And if we kept them here, it would give me a reason to talk to Fred.

I left Jeanette a message saying I'd take care of the whatsits for the night, then shoved my laptop and all the papers on my desk into my backpack.

"Nice try, but I'm still beating you out the door," John said with a laugh as he hefted his duffel bag.

"Says the man who works 'part time'." I made quotes in

the air as I spoke. I'd been there eleven hours without a break, and John had arrived before me. "Hang on a sec." I leaned out of the office and waved to catch Christopher's attention. When he looked up, I asked, "Can you drive all of us to my place? I walked to work today."

Christopher gave me a thumbs-up sign and went back to his call.

John laughed. "Your car still hasn't aired out?"

"It was a nice day," I protested. "Walking is good exercise." A brindlelion had sprayed my car weeks ago, and the upholstery still reeked. "Go home and calm some beef for those poor orphans."

"Whatever you say, boss." John walked out the back door, singing a Louis Armstrong song as he went.

6

By the time I'd returned from letting the receptionists know I was leaving, Christopher was huddled over his phone with Fred, working out how to use the translation app. He looked up when I came over. "Change of plans. The director wants us to take him to a hotel. They have a team coming out tomorrow to fly him to the verdiran embassy in New York. They'll collect him from the hotel in the morning."

"No."

He quirked one brow. "No?"

"No." I leaned against the wall and crossed my arms. "He came in with a collapsed lung this morning. He can't fly safely for weeks. If he'd rather stay at a hotel, that's fine, but someone needs to be available in case he has trouble breathing again. Are you volunteering to put in a chest tube in the middle of the night if he needs it? I'll give you all the supplies, if you want."

Christopher's eyes widened and he drew back. Then he blew out his breath in a laugh. "I thought you were serious there for a second."

"Until someone else takes over, he's *my* patient." I nodded at the phone. "Ask him what *he* wants to do."

Fred watched us as we spoke. He handed the phone to Christopher, as if requesting an explanation. Christopher nodded once. "I'll find out."

"Do we know what his name really is?"

"I asked that, but his answer isn't getting translated."

He'd have to continue as Fred for now. While Christopher worked on determining where Fred wanted to spend the night, I transferred the sleeping babies into a carrier. Since I didn't know how often they needed to be fed, I'd have to err on the side of caution. And if they got dehydrated overnight, I'd give them another fluid bolus. Plus, they might help me ask Fred questions.

By the time I'd finished, Christopher had his reply. "*Fred*," he said, stumbling over the name, "would like to go to your house."

"Excellent." I shouldered my backpack and lifted the carrier. "Are we ready?"

Christopher sighed. "My boss is going to kill me." He pulled his keys from his pocket. "I'll bring the truck close to the door."

∾

WE DROVE to my house and Christopher pulled his truck in behind my Civic. As we helped Fred move along the sidewalk toward the path to the front door, the smell of brindle-lion urine wafted over to us. Christopher leaned forward a little so he could look past Fred to me. "Doesn't really seem to be wearing off, does it?"

I'd washed my car three times myself and taken it to the detailing place once. Every time, it seemed a little better until I drove it again. "I don't know what you're talking about. I don't smell anything." When he opened his mouth, I cut in. "It's not the air filter." Every man I talked to wanted to explain air filters to me. I'd already changed the air filter twice.

"I was just going to say my cousin could probably fix it, if you want me to call her. She's got a gift."

"I'm sure it will stop smelling soon."

"Suit yourself. You have my number if you change your mind."

I gave him a sideways glance to see if that was a dig about me having his number for a few weeks and not calling, but he was busy showing Fred the zap lizard nest in the gutter above my front door.

By nine o'clock, I was sitting on my couch, Christopher beside me, three baby whatsits in a carrier by my feet, and the remains of the red dragon family special from Jade Palace on my coffee table.

Fred was ensconced in my hideous recliner to keep his leg elevated. His green skin clashed with the chair's orange and brown stripes, but somehow he seemed to fit, as if he belonged to whatever world had created that fabric. He looked more at home than I did.

Christopher looked around the living room. "You have a nice place."

"Thanks." Only because he'd said something, I actually *saw* my living room for the first time in a long while. Everything was clean — if I didn't keep on top of that, I knew Antonia would take care of it, and she already did too many things for me. But I hadn't changed anything in years. The house was just the place where I came to collapse until it was time to go to work again.

Lately, I'd been feeling like maybe that wasn't quite enough.

Dumbo and Twitter, my two cats, were locked in my bedroom to keep them out of the food. Taco, the fist-sized gremlin, flitted around the room, going from person to person. She'd been excited I was home, delighted to see Christopher again, and very curious about the verdiran. Fred clicked to her and scratched the top of her head, clearly familiar with gremlins.

Fred and Christopher had been handing the phone back and forth during dinner, so now we knew Fred liked the sweet and sour pork, and was grateful for the hospitality. Our attempts to apologize for any offense we might give through ignorance had been flicked aside.

"He doesn't *seem* particularly formal," I said, as I watched the verdiran play peek-a-boo with Taco. If we'd offended him at any point in the last few hours, it hadn't been obvious. "What am I missing?"

Christopher looked as confused as I felt. "I have no idea."

Fred scooped up the gremlin and put her on his shoulder so he had room to open up his satchel. After rummaging through it, he brought out a newspaper clipping, wrinkled and yellowing.

I recognized the picture. "That's..." *Me.* Fred had an article with a picture of *me*.

I crossed the room and took the paper from him to be sure. The clipping was six months old, from a local article about the veterinary hospital just after we'd been awarded one of the first federal grants to study xenotic physiology.

It was supposed to have been all about the changes in the hospital, and our switch to seeing more xenotic patients. But by the time it came out, the article had turned into a sappy piece about the plucky veterinarian who had lost her husband in the portal storms and now bravely treated xenotics.

When I'd complained, the reporter claimed his editor made him change the slant of the piece. Then he'd sold it to a national magazine, and for two days the hospital had received an onslaught of interview requests from other media outlets. By that time, I'd learned my lesson about trusting reporters. They still called when there was a xenotics biology question in the news, but they never wanted to pay me for my time.

The article had been accompanied by a picture of me

examining a roc, one of the new green-throated variety that had shown up for the first time a few weeks before. The keratin spikes over her spine and her stubby wings made her look like a chubby, cat-sized dragon. That look had led to a fad of roc owners posing their pets with knight dolls and miniature castles. Rocs looked imposing until they opened their mouths and whined for attention.

Now Fred tapped the picture and flipped his palm so all five fingers were pointing at me.

I nodded. "Yes, that's me." Belatedly, I tapped my fingers against the opposite palm.

Christopher moved to my side. "May I?" He took the article from me and scanned it.

"Please don't read that. The article's crap. Why would Fred have it?" Having Christopher read the sappy pull quotes made me want to disappear through the floor. "It has to be something about the picture." Fred wouldn't be able to read the words.

"Let's find out." Christopher handed the article back to Fred and typed on his phone, trying to find some combination of words that produced script instead of the asterisks that meant the app couldn't translate his sentence.

I gathered the empty plates so I wouldn't be tempted to stand behind him and tell him what to type. "This would be easier if we had that app installed on more than one device." He glanced over with a smile, but didn't take the bait. "I'm going to go see if my mother-in-law still has her crutches. Be right back." I dropped off the plates in the sink, then went out the kitchen door toward the building that had once been the garage and now was Antonia's tiny apartment.

The backyard was an oasis of calm, a feat achieved entirely by Antonia and her love of gardening. Rechargeable lights glowed along the paving stone walkway that undulated toward the other side of the property. Later in the summer, the raised beds lining the walkway would have an abundance of tomatoes, peppers, and other vegetables I looked forward to, but right now, kale and chard dominated. They were pretty, but the tiny gremlin ate more of them than I did.

Antonia answered the door with gauzy green fabric draped over her tie-dyed t-shirt and slacks. Her short gray hair was tucked under a green felt hat, and cloth leaves were pinned in strategic places. "Nessa! Come in! Have you eaten yet? Katie and I were just working on our Spring Fest costumes."

"Hi, Katie." Stepping inside, I waved at the purple-haired woman standing in the living room. "I don't want to interrupt. I just came by to see if you still had those crutches." No way was I getting in the middle of this. Last year, Antonia had worn an amazingly detailed birch tree costume, only to lose first prize to "that hagfish, Dolores", who had been wearing little more than a corset and body paint. The senior center spring queen voting committee was made up entirely of men. This year Antonia's approach hinted at the adage "if you can't beat 'em, join 'em."

Antonia turned and opened the closet that held the vacuum and everything else long and skinny, then plucked out two aluminum crutches. "Is everything okay?" She glanced at my legs as she handed the crutches over.

"I'm fine. These are for a..." I stumbled over what to call Fred. "A patient, I guess. There's an injured verdiran staying at my place tonight, Fred, so don't worry if you see someone else moving around in the house. He seems nice enough, but he doesn't speak English." Actually, I wasn't sure a verdiran even *could* speak English. I hadn't heard him make any sounds that suggested a human-like larynx.

Antonia moved to the window so she could look across the yard to my house. "Really? And who's *that*?"

I moved so I could see through the window. Christopher was walking along the path, my phone in his hand. "That's the DPAS ranger. He's here to make sure we don't cause a diplomatic incident." I opened the door and went outside.

Christopher handed me my phone. "Someone called twice, and I thought it might be important..."

"Thanks." Only after I had tapped the screen to call back did I realize Antonia had followed me out the door. "Christopher, this is Antonia." Then the receptionist at the emergency clinic answered, and I moved away to concentrate on what she was saying. By the time I'd been transferred to the clinician who needed help, told her which drugs should be safe to sedate a gremlin, and returned, Antonia and Christopher had moved past introductions and were discussing who might be able to replicate gingerbread trim for his house.

I held up the crutches. "Thanks for these. I'm going to get back inside to make sure Fred's okay." Not that I was worried about Fred suddenly decompensating. I just wanted to postpone Antonia's questions about Christopher. There was no way she wouldn't have recognized his name — I'd told her about the hike a few weeks ago.

Antonia smiled. "Good night, sweetheart. I'll see you in the morning. It was nice to meet you, Christopher."

Yep. She'd be grilling me about this soon. Oh well. At least I'd get a good breakfast out of it.

Christopher caught up with me as I hurried back to the house. "So now I've met your mother-in-law."

"I warned you she would have opinions about your home remodel." Buying a Victorian that needed restoration was not for the faint of heart.

"You did. And she does." He paused. "Does she always dress so... eclectically?"

"The tie-dye, yes. The dress on top, no. Our senior center holds a Spring Fest every year, and..." Explaining the all-out competitiveness of a group of seniors who accumulated grudges like other people saved grocery bags seemed too involved, so I waved the hand not holding the crutches. "It's a thing. You have to see it to understand."

"Right." He lengthened his stride in order to climb the porch stairs first so he could hold the kitchen door open for me. "I called my boss and pointed out you might need to communicate with our friend if there was a medical emergency. He agreed to let me install the translation app on your tablet."

I slanted a look as I went inside. "Did you tell him we named him Fred?"

"Absolutely not."

Back in the living room, Fred was drawing in his notebook while he and Taco carried on a whistling conversation. When I demonstrated the crutches, his eyes lit up and he stood. After I'd dumped the contents of my backpack to find my tablet, Fred and I adjusted the height of the crutches while Christopher set up the app for me.

The verdiran examined the screw and wing nut combination curiously, but he quickly figured out their use and two minutes later I was showing him the guest bathroom. While I was at that end of the hall, I let the cats out of my bedroom so they would quit scratching at the door. Twitter raced down the hallway to the carrier with the baby whatsits, sniffed once, then hissed and ran back into the bedroom. Dumbo trotted down the hall two steps in front of me, chirruping to remind me that her food dish might need more kibble.

When I got back to the living room, Christopher held up the envelope with the CF logo. His expression was guarded. "Do you work with the Chevalier Foundation?"

My knee-jerk reaction was to respond with, *Do you always go through other people's mail?* But there was an edge of worry about his question that threw me off. "No. They offered me a job a few weeks ago and seem to have a hard time accepting my refusal. Why? Do you have experience with them?"

"They've hired a lot of DPAS personnel in the last year. And they've been sending me job offers lately."

"They must be expanding."

I assumed there was more to his troubled look, but he distracted me by handing over the tablet. "It's all installed. Try not to ask anything that's going to get me fired."

I gave him my best insincere smile. "Of course not."

He stood up. "What time do you normally go to work in the morning?"

"Between six-thirty and seven."

He nodded. "I doubt the team coming to pick up Fred will get here before then. Do you want me to drive you?"

"No. I'll take my car." At his suspiciously blank look at the ceiling, I glared. "It doesn't smell that bad." It really *did* smell that bad, but I needed time to get all the information I could out of the verdiran, without anyone from DPAS worried I would offend him.

"Air filter," he whispered, and then he laughed. "Just kidding. If you change your mind about letting my cousin help, text me. I'll drop by your hospital to help with Fred in the morning." When Fred swung down the hallway, Christopher used his phone to explain he was leaving for the night. I waved goodbye, and Fred copied the gesture.

I forced myself to close the door behind him instead of watching him walk all the way to his truck.

Fred dropped into the recliner, at which point Dumbo jumped on top of him and wandered down his leg to sniff the cast. Since Fred didn't seem bothered, I let the cat do her thing, pulled a chair closer, and tried to figure out how to ask what I needed to know. But Fred had his own agenda. He took the tablet and tapped at the screen. Holding up the newspaper article, he pointed to the English translation. "*When?*"

The picture had been taken a while ago, and I had to look up the records on the green-throated roc. Then the date just gave asterisks instead of a translation, so I brought over the wall calendar covering the damaged plaster in the kitchen and flipped to the year view. After a few minutes, he grasped the concept, and I circled the day the roc had been brought in. He scribbled in his notebook, doing something that looked a lot like calculations. In the end, he drew a box around something he'd written, but he didn't try to translate it, so it seemed to be for his own purposes.

The app nearly defeated me with its failures, but I kept simplifying and restating questions until I finally got down to the bare minimum. Pointing at the whatsits sleeping in their carrier, I gestured to the translation with my other hand. "*How big?*"

If they stayed fairly small, it wouldn't be too hard to find a zoo or wildlife rehabber who could set aside space. But if they grew to the size of grizzly bears, the options would rapidly dwindle. Ideally, we would be able to send them back to the place they'd come from, though even that posed risks. What if they carried back novel bacteria from this world? I'd have been more concerned about contamination if there hadn't already been a link between their world and ours. That ship had sailed.

Fred held his hand about a foot from the floor, then pointed to Dumbo, who was sprawled over his legs.

Okay, so roughly house cat sized. I could work with that.

Fred tried a dozen times to ask something, but none of the translations came through. He turned to a fresh page in his notebook and drew something.

Squinting at the drawing, I angled my head and decided it was supposed to be a roc. "Sorry, buddy. Your drawing skills aren't much better than mine." I pointed from his notebook to the newspaper article and he tapped *yes*. His forehead wrinkled, though I couldn't tell if he was laughing at his own drawing or my inability to interpret it.

After messing around with the app for a few minutes, I decided it either didn't allow users to add words or I didn't have access to that feature. I took the pencil from him and wrote *roc* next to the drawing on his notebook. When he started shading the picture, I went to the kitchen junk drawer. Antonia probably had crayons or colored pencils and would know exactly where they were. The only things I could find were pink and yellow highlighters, but Fred seemed delighted when I brought them back. He used the yellow highlighter to color in a patch on the roc's throat. Then he drew another roc, even less realistic than the last, and colored its wingtips yellow.

"Have I seen a roc with green wingtips?" I thought about it. "Maybe?" There had been so many xenotics that came through the hospital that I lost track. But if Fred was looking for specific animals, I had something better than my memory. I retrieved my laptop and brought up the xenotic photo album.

At work, I took pictures of everything and connected

them to the chart — if something came up later, I'd have a record. So my photo roll was an eye-blistering cascade of wounds and scars, but if Fred was looking for something specific, it would likely be somewhere in there. He just needed enough patience to look through it all. Someday I was going to get organized and add keywords to everything, but today was not that day.

After a short tutorial on how to scroll, zoom, and pan, he came back with his earlier question. "*When?*" My explanation of the date format required a lot of pointing to the calendar, but when I wrote out the month number next to all the months in the year-view, he quickly caught on. After he successfully puzzled out one date on his own, I left him to look through pictures while I dug out my old laptop. It didn't work without being plugged in, which was why I'd upgraded, but it would be good enough for writing up the day's charts.

While the old laptop was booting, I figured it was time to ask my most important question. If Fred left with the DPAS team tomorrow, I'd never get another chance. Using the back of a flier, I drew the terrain Christopher and I had seen when we'd gone to another world while fleeing the goliath, with ranks of portals in an obvious pattern. I added a large snake looking through one portal, and a shaggy thing with horns, the closest I could get to drawing a goliath. Then I added a stick figure that could have been a human but was supposed to be a verdiran.

Leaning over to place the paper on top of the keyboard, I gave him a chance to take it in. Then I pointed from the verdiran on the paper to Fred. "Was that you?" I tapped my fingers for yes, slapped my palm down for no. "Yes or no?"

If Fred was the verdiran I'd seen, he knew how to navigate between the worlds, and maybe he could help us find some of the people who had disappeared. Maybe he could tell me if Mark was dead or alive.

The verdiran stared at me for a few seconds, and from his focus I had the feeling I'd startled him. Or maybe even scared him. Finally, he slapped his palm down. So that hadn't been him I'd seen. Then he pointed to the translation app, which still had the last thing he'd asked. "*When?*" All traces of laughter had left his face.

I tapped the date of the hike on the calendar. "Three weeks ago."

He folded the picture carefully until it was small enough to slip between two pages of his book. His next translation took a few tries before he handed over the tablet. "*Danger. Secret.*"

Then he went back to scrolling through pictures and refused to answer any more questions.

8

T he next morning I woke to the sound of Antonia talking in the kitchen. If I had closed the bedroom door, I wouldn't have been able to hear her, but I'd left the door open so I could hear the sleigh bells I'd given Fred to ring if he was having difficulty breathing overnight. I'd asked him twice how the lung injury had happened, but he either didn't understand the question or didn't want to talk about it. I could only hope it was a one-time event.

Since Antonia's conversations with the cats and gremlin usually had shorter sentences, I assumed she was talking to Fred. True, there was no way Fred understood her, but that wouldn't bother Antonia.

After a shower, more awake but still hoping to avoid her questions about Christopher, I listened from the living room as Antonia instructed Fred on the proper amount of cheese to grate. "Just a little more. This much." Then her voice rose. "Good morning, Nessa. There's coffee, if you want some."

Busted. I smiled as I walked into the kitchen. "Good morning." All three whatsit babies were growling and scratching at something in their carrier — Fred had fed them. Taco perched on the corner of the cupboard, watching all the activity, probably waiting until we were distracted to fly down and steal something from the cutting board.

My smile slipped a bit as I took in Fred's attire. In a fit of expediency, I'd taken all Mark's clothes, untouched since he'd disappeared four years ago, and put them in the guest bedroom for Fred to use. Mark and Fred were roughly the same size, and *someone* might as well get some use out of them. But now I was watching this alien stranger seated at the table Mark and I had found at a garage sale, wearing shorts and a t-shirt from a band we'd seen on one of our first dates, and... I took a careful breath.

Antonia pressed my "All bleeding stops... eventually" mug into my hands. "It was a good step," she murmured. Then her voice took on its usual cheerful tone. "Is there any food Fred can't eat?"

"Not as far as I know." When Fred looked up from his careful grating, I exaggerated my breathing. "Yes?"

He made a thumbs-up sign, which startled a laugh out of me. That had to be Antonia's doing — I hadn't taught him that. "Good."

Antonia pushed me toward a chair, then went back to the stove. She let me take one sip of coffee before saying, "Christopher seems nice."

"You know he was just here to help with Fred, right?" I took another sip. "He works for DPAS."

Antonia would know what I meant by that. Mark had disappeared in the initial portal storm, that wild night the portals had first appeared. During storms, the portals didn't stay in one location, but manifested and swept in everyone along their path, until they went away seconds or minutes later. There had only been a few storms, and the portals currently appeared and disappeared in the same location. Still, instead of avoiding portals like any sane person, Christopher sought them out. In his last position, he'd even led teams to map the territory on the other side.

"He seems pretty level-headed to me. With his knowledge, he probably knows how to be careful."

I stared at her. She stared back until I dropped my gaze.

"First, we start by cracking eggs into a bowl," she told Fred, suiting actions to words.

Last night I hadn't had eggs or any of the items neatly chopped on the cutting board. Antonia did most of my shopping, because she didn't think Count Chocula cereal for breakfast and dinner was healthy. My take was that it was fortified with vitamins and minerals, and if I drank the occasional glass of orange juice, I wouldn't get scurvy either.

As she melted butter in the pan, Antonia kept up her instructions to Fred, occasionally throwing in a question for me. "Then we add the cheese, like this. If Fred stays here, it will be nice to have Christopher just a few blocks away, won't it?"

All the subtlety of a sledgehammer.

"I don't think Fred's staying. There's a team from DPAS flying out to take care of him today." Fred couldn't fly, but if they wanted to take him to the east coast, there was no reason they couldn't go on an extended road trip.

If he wanted to go.

Last night Fred had compiled a list of things in his notebook related to the xenotics I'd photographed and the dates they'd come to the hospital. At least, I was pretty sure that's what he had been doing. While I couldn't read his body language clearly, he was worried about something. I'd finally shooed him back down the hall to the guest bedroom to get some sleep.

So I didn't know why the verdiran was here, or why he'd been trying to find out when that roc had been in the hospital. But he knew something about navigating the portals. I just had to figure out how to get him to tell me.

"Now we put the lid on for a bit to let it set. Maybe we should organize a neighborhood work day when we could all go over and help him with the house."

Dumbo jumped on my lap, sniffed my coffee, and sneezed."Maybe we should let him fix the dry rot in the floors first."

"Good point. Still." She turned to face me, one hand on the lid. "You *could* just invite him to dinner." Then she hastily added, "I'll cook."

"I'll think about it." Something about Christopher's expression when he'd seen the envelope from the Chevalier Foundation bothered me. When Antonia looked over, I feigned an offended look. "I'll *think* about it."

"Good." She split the omelet between two plates and set them in front of Fred and me. "Now, do you need me to give you two a ride to work today, or is Christopher coming back to pick you up?"

"I'm taking my car."

Antonia sighed. "Nessa..."

My car really didn't smell that bad. Not compared to how it had been a few weeks ago, anyhow. It probably would have been fine already if I'd been able to leave the windows open, but the neighborhood cats kept going inside to sniff the upholstery, and a zap lizard had tried to make a nest on the dashboard.

Fred visibly recoiled when I opened the passenger door,

but his forehead wrinkled. I helped him move the seat all the way back, and then he folded himself inside with the crutches in front of him. I helped him buckle the seatbelt, closed the door, and ran around to the other side so I could start the car and show him how the windows worked.

Like most spring mornings, the air was chilly and the seats quickly sucked away the warmth. From long experience, I knew the car's heater would be useless until we reached the halfway point, the only traffic light on the route I usually took. Fred had his window open a crack. He sat up so his nose was closer to the fresh air.

"It's better than it was," I said. We stopped at the red light and waited for it to complete its cycle. Something had gone wrong with the pavement sensors — it gave time to left turns, then cars and pedestrians going perpendicular, then left turns for the forward traffic, and finally anyone driving through, again with the pedestrian count-down. Back before the portal storms, there had been enough traffic in the mornings that nobody would have noticed it wasn't sensing vehicles. Now, it meant a three-minute wait when there were no other cars around.

A blast of acrid brindlelion odor came from the vents when I turned on the heater. Fred coughed, opened his window all the way, and leaned his head out.

"It's not that bad!" Dammit, I was going to have to call Christopher's cousin.

As the light finally turned green, Fred shifted the satchel he held on his lap. When I reflexively checked left for traffic, I saw a portal on the center median wink out of existence.

Adrenaline made my skin tingle. If a portal showed up in the roadway while we were moving forward, we would go through it, ending up who knows where. In the very best case, I'd be able to reverse and come back through. In the worst case, we'd end up in water or at the edge of a cliff and die. I moved my foot from the brake to the accelerator and we moved into the intersection.

If portals were randomly showing up in town, maybe it was time to leave.

9

When we arrived at the hospital, I spent two seconds soaking up the pre-chaos calm, then transferred the whatsits to a cage. John had already come in and gone out on a farm call, but he'd left dehydrated ribs in the refrigerator. With Fred's approval, I put one in the cage with the babies. Three seconds later, tiny teeth crunched bits of bone. Finding a home for these things when they grew bigger might take some effort.

I held up my stethoscope and pointed at Fred's chest. "Can I?" He nodded, another gesture he'd picked up from Antonia.

It felt odd to have a patient who understood why I was doing what I did. Normally, I kept one eye on my patient to watch for any signs of violence and kept my movements quiet, so I didn't startle them. Now I had Fred watching me while I worked. Closing my eyes, I listened to his breathing. "Everything sounds good." I opened my eyes and gave him the thumbs-up.

Rochelle pushed through the door to the treatment room. "Hi, Fred!" She waved at him and he waved back.

Then she turned to me. "Dr. C, there's a woman out front holding a pigamus that got caught in barbed wire. Emergency clinic?"

According to the clock, we didn't open for another hour. But the doctors at the emergency clinic would be busy transferring patients so they could close in ninety minutes. There was a good chance they would just send the owner right back here. "Put her in a room and get her information. I'll come up and grab the pigamus." Someday I'd have a calm morning where I could sit at my desk with a cup of coffee and get through the stack of pathology reports, but today was not that day.

The pigamus had severed an artery. Lucky for him, it was a small one, but by the time I got Kermit stabilized, blood had misted Fred's shirt and splattered across my face. Rochelle came back as I was suturing. She blinked when she saw me. "You have a little, uh..." She gestured at her own face.

I tied the knot and moved to the next laceration, adjusting Fred's grip on the leg so I had a good angle. "Tell mom things are going well and Kermit might be ready to go home around lunchtime." I'd only spoken a few words to the woman as I'd taken Kermit from her — Rochelle had written up the estimate and had her sign authorization forms. I was thankful Fred had been willing to help — the last time I'd needed an owner's assistance during an emergency, the man had passed out when he saw the needle.

Rochelle nodded. "Sounds good. Also... Ranger Garcia is in the waiting area with a group of people from DPAS for Fred." She checked over her shoulder and her brows lifted. "Or, actually, I guess they're here now."

I shrugged. Rochelle would have asked them to wait; if

they ignored her and came back here, any squeamishness was their problem.

When Rochelle moved out of the way, three people in suits came through the door. I didn't recognize the woman or the first man, but Christopher brought up the rear, looking faintly apologetic. His eyes widened when he saw my face. Then Fred waved to him with his free hand, and Christopher blinked. He waved back.

The man at the front moved so he was more or less in front of Fred, which put him across the treatment table from the sedated pigamus and near my left elbow. From the corner of my eye, I saw him bow and make some complicated motion with his hands. Fred waved.

The other stranger — presumably a junior assistant based on her age and deference — froze. So maybe Fred really wasn't as formal as the other verdirans, and the document hadn't been wrong.

Christopher moved around the assistant. He looked good in a suit, but it also made him look like he belonged somewhere else. "Director Noonan, this is Dr. Cunningham. She's been responsible for the verdiran's medical care since he arrived." He'd hesitated slightly before he said "the verdiran", as if considering calling him Fred and then deciding against it. Coward.

I trimmed the ragged edges of the pigamus's skin and dabbed it with gauze, considering if I needed to do something to relieve the tension on this suture line. "Nice to meet you. I'd shake your hand, but we have about five minutes before Kermit realizes what's going on and I'd like to be done before then."

"Of course." Director Noonan's voice could have frozen boiling water. Then he ignored me and held up a page of text for Fred to read.

I tied the final knot, pushed at the skin, and added a couple shallow incisions parallel to my line of sutures. The needle drivers clanged against the metal stand as I swapped them for bandage material. Across the table, Fred shook his head.

When I looked up, the assistant's eyes had grown wider.

The director's voice kept its chill. "Perhaps Ranger Garcia could assist here while I discuss travel plans with the verdiran?" He gestured toward the back hallway, and Christopher took off his suit jacket and moved forward to take over leg holding duty.

I waited until they had all moved away. "Super friendly guy, your boss."

"More like my boss's boss's boss, except I think there's another three levels in there. I don't think he usually makes these sorts of trips himself."

"So why's he here?"

Christopher glanced over his shoulder. "Damage control. In case someone finds out they brought a verdiran to an animal hospital."

Near my right elbow, Kermit lifted his head. "Don't let him fall off the table." I finished the first bandage and moved to the other leg. "So I guess that means I won't be getting a medal for helping Fred."

Christopher winced. "Probably a safe assumption."

Whatever. I didn't need recognition from the DPAS. My clients brought me chocolate every December. Sometimes we even got homemade cookies.

The assistant walked by, phone to her ear. She looked around, saw us, then moved toward the hallway that led to the break room.

I kept my voice low. "Fred's not cooperating." As I bandaged, I considered telling Christopher what Fred had said. *Danger. Secret.* No, that wasn't a conversation we could have now. Not when I didn't know why there was danger or who it needed to be a secret from.

Kermit tried to stand up in earnest. I unfurled a towel near my feet and scooped up the pigamus.

"Let me help you..." Christopher trailed off as I lowered Kermit to the floor.

"He's only forty pounds. No need to get your nice shirt dirty." I crouched on the floor to finish bandaging. Now that he was on the ground, Kermit relaxed again.

The back door slammed shut. In the hallway, Laurie said, "Hi, Fred. Excuse me. I just need to get by. Thanks." She was shaking her head when she got to the treatment room. "Who's that guy...?" Then one hand flew up to cover her mouth. "Dr. C, you... Hang on, let me put my bag down, and you can go wash up."

Fred came back to stand by the treatment table. He began cleaning up the area, throwing the bloody gauze into the trash and moving the instruments into the sink. Apparently, he'd been paying attention to how things worked the day before.

Director Noonan followed him, tablet in hand, but Fred ignored him. Noonan's lips thinned. "Is there a room we can use while we arrange a call with the verdiran embassy?"

"Here." I opened the door to room four, then locked the connecting door to the waiting area.

Director Noonan's nostrils flared when he saw the size of the exam room, but he didn't comment. At least the room had been thoroughly cleaned since the last time any animals had been there, and only faintly smelled of anal glands.

With seven animals coming in for surgery this morning, I had seven clients to reassure in the next hour. On top of that, John would be seeing appointments. We didn't have extra space in the building.

In the hallway, I tapped Moira's arm as she worked to fill prescription requests that had come in overnight. "DPAS is using room four for a while, so we'll have to make do with the other three."

"Sounds good — Ah!" She turned as she was talking and recoiled with a laugh. "Dr. C, you need to clean up before you admit your patients." She pushed me toward the bathroom. "Go!"

The bathroom mirror informed me I had blood smeared across one cheek and my forehead. No wonder everyone had been giving me strange looks. I washed my face and pulled on a new scrub top. When I went back out, Moira smiled.

"Much better. Mrs. Podgorski is in one with Tulip, Ms. Larkin is in two with Baghie, and Mr. Cole is in three with Doggy."

Since these were all planned surgeries, Moira would have already had them sign estimates. As long as none of the owners had too many last-minute questions, I would be in surgery by eight-thirty.

The door to room four opened, and Director Noonan stepped out. "Dr. Cunningham. A moment of your time, please."

The sooner I got them out of here, the better. I caught Moira's eye. "If I'm not out in five minutes, come get me," I murmured.

"If you're not out in five minutes, the clients will riot," she replied.

That made me smile as I went into the exam room. It felt even more crowded than it should be with the three people from DPAS standing, plus Fred seated on the bench, his crutches propped against the wall. Christopher looked up at the ceiling, so I directed my words to Noonan. "What can I do for you?"

His perfect posture didn't change, but I had the feeling he was forcing out words against his will. "The ambassador would be... pleased if you would continue to offer hospitality to this verdiran. Allowing him to stay in your home and accompany you to work."

Keep Fred around long enough to get answers about the portals? That had been my goal. But there was no sense in appearing too eager. "For how long?"

The assistant stared at me. Maybe nobody ever questioned her boss. Christopher continued to pretend he was just a bystander, waiting in this room for something else to occur. Noonan's lips thinned. "That wasn't determined." He paused. "There would be a stipend."

He thought I needed to be bribed. Good. "We would need to have that translation app available for everyone."

"Of course. I'll make sure you have everything you need."

The grouping of the people in the room suddenly made sense. Noonan and his assistant were separating themselves from Christopher, and Christopher was trying not to appear... too eager? Too close to me? Probably the latter. DPAS seemed very cliquish, and the director wanted control over everything. Noonan had tried to physically bring Fred back to New York. Now that had failed, and he wanted to retain all control from afar, so he was cutting Christopher out of the loop.

But I was betting I could change that. "Do you have a number where I can reach you if I have any questions? I noticed there were a lot of things that didn't get translated, and that might cause problems, especially if it's the middle of the night and we're at the emergency clinic."

Noonan's gaze flicked over to Fred for the first time since I'd entered the room. "I understood the verdiran's medical condition had been dealt with."

"What? Oh, yeah, he's fine. I meant when we're at the emergency clinic to treat patients." I cocked my head. "You said he was supposed to go with me to work, right? I'm on call four nights a week. So I'll need someone to talk to if we run into issues." I paused for a moment to let Noonan imagine constant calls about inconsequential things in the middle of the night. "Or should I just call Ranger Garcia since he's local?"

Noonan's eyes narrowed as he looked at me. As long as Fred wanted me, Noonan was stuck. I was perfectly capable of calling him or his assistants every half hour to ask stupid questions, and he knew it. "Yes. Ranger Garcia should be your first point of contact." He gave Christopher a dour look. "You'll keep me informed."

Christopher nodded.

I gave my this-appointment-is-over-unless-you-have-other-concerns smile. "Great. Do you need me for anything else? I have patients to admit."

10

S urgery mornings were always my favorites. The steady beep of the pulse oximeter provided a soothing soundtrack as I searched for the musk slinky's left ovary. About a quarter of them didn't have two ovaries, and it looked like this was one of those. I pushed the intestines to the side so I could get a better look.

The DPAS group had gone soon after I'd agreed to house Fred. Christopher had come back half an hour later, and now he and Fred were in the break room with a pile of electronics that Christopher was teaching Fred to use.

Rochelle knocked on the frame of the open door. "Dr. C? Can I talk at you?"

"What's up?" Aha! There it was, smaller than the right ovary and just barely attached to a vestigial uterine horn.

"There's a Kirk Mullins from the Chevalier Foundation up front." When I looked up in surprised, she nodded. "He says he's in the area for the day and wanted to know if you had a few minutes to talk." After a pause, she added, "Your afternoon appointments are all booked."

I'd be lucky if every slot wasn't double-booked. Tying off

the minuscule artery, I wondered what would bring the technical director of the foundation out to River Terrace. He couldn't possibly have flown across the country to talk to me without making an appointment. Maybe he had business in Sacramento. "Do you think he'll quit bugging me if I see him?"

Rochelle shrugged. "I can get rid of him, if you want."

It was a tempting thought, but I suspected he'd just keep contacting me. "No, go ahead and bring him back."

Rochelle nodded once. "Will do."

By the time she came back with a tall white man whose receding hairline evoked a monk's tonsure, I had switched suture. "I'm closing the skin," I warned Kathleen, who monitored the musk slinky's vitals at the head of the surgery table. She dialed down the anesthetic and made a note on her chart.

Rochelle knocked on the door frame. "Dr. C, this is Kirk Mullins."

"Thanks, Rochelle." I briefly made eye contact with the man, then looked down at my suture line. "You're very persistent."

"And you're a tough nut to crack," he said, a slight twang to his words. "I had business in town and I thought I'd come by and see if you might be free for lunch. My treat!"

"This is as free as I get. I appreciate the job offer, but..."

"Now, now, don't be too hasty." He took half a step forward, as if he were going to come into the operating room, then thought better of it. "Maybe if we talked a bit, I'd find some way to sweeten the deal."

I clipped off the final suture and pulled away the drape. "Kathleen, I'll take over here so you can help Laurie get Baghie prepped." After disconnecting the endotracheal tube so the musk slinky was breathing room air, I freed her limbs. "Mr. Mullins, —"

"Call me Kirk."

I gave him points for trying. "Kirk, there are plenty of other veterinarians out there who would be perfect for that position."

"Not ones who have the xenotics experience we're looking for," he said. "Whenever I ask people to name the top veterinarians in the field, your name always comes up."

He obviously meant it to be flattering, but the xenotics community was so small, it wasn't as impressive as it might seem. The universities had been slow to create new departments, so most of the information was coming from private practitioners, and my hospital happened to be in a place that saw a lot of different xenotics come through. "Even so, I can give you some names if you want them. Casey Freeman is about to finish a fellowship, and I don't know what her plans are after that." The musk slinky raised her head, so I stopped to pull the endotracheal tube before she could chew on it.

Kirk shook his head. "I'm set on you, Vanessa. Work with me here. What can I offer that might change your..." His voice trailed off. "But that's..."

Through the OR door, I saw Fred and Christopher standing on the other side of the treatment room, looking at the tablet in Christopher's hands.

"Oh, that's Fred. He's here to help out for a bit."

"Fred?" Somehow he sounded even more startled by the name than he had been by the verdiran's presence.

Right. We needed to find out what Fred's real name was before it turned into an incident. "It's a temporary name while we're trying to figure out how to translate his real one." The musk slinky made a wobbly attempt to get to her feet, so I scooped her up and walked past Kirk into the treatment room. Once I'd wrapped her in a blanket and settled her in a cage, I stripped off my gloves and pulled my mask down. "Kirk, I appreciate the offer. I really do. But I'm just not interested."

Maybe he finally heard something in my tone, because that seemed to do it. He smiled, though this time the smile didn't reach his eyes, as if I was seeing how he looked at people he wasn't trying to persuade. "Well, if you change your mind, you know how to get in touch. Thank you for your time." He turned and walked through the door toward the reception area.

I watched him go, confused. He'd come all the way out here, insisted on seeing me, and then suddenly dropped the matter. Maybe he was phobic about verdirans. If he was, he was in the wrong position. I shrugged and checked on the musk slinky. She'd gone back to sleep, but the tip of her tongue stuck out and it was a well-oxygenated pink.

Christopher's voice broke into my thoughts. "Nessa, do you have a second?"

Laurie and Kathleen were still working on the IV catheter for my next patient. "As long as it's quick."

"Let me show you how to create a session before I leave, so you and Fred don't have to be looking at the same device."

"We can text?"

"Uh, yeah, I guess that's a way to look at it." He gestured with his chin toward the door Mullins had left through. "Sounded like another job offer. You're popular."

"Same offer, but I think seeing Fred threw him off his game." After a quick glance to make sure the musk slinky was still recovering well, I looked down at the tablet he was holding. "Okay, show me how this works."

11

T he last clients were checking out in reception when the back door opened and Jeanette came in, holding a carrier and clipboard.

I held my arms open. "Officer Dyer, you come bearing gifts! Another two minutes and you would have missed me." Not actually true, but technically, we'd been closed for fifteen minutes.

"Sorry. It's been a long day." She glanced at Fred. "The jolly green giant looks healthy." She waved at him and he mirrored her greeting. Her face paled. "Shit, tell me he doesn't understand English," she whispered.

I put my phone down on the counter and took the carrier from her. "You're off the hook. All we have right now is a translation app. Someone surrendered this guy?" I peered into the carrier and saw a roc huddled in the corner, its head tucked under one vestigial wing. His fur had a slight green tinge, so most likely an immature male. The keratin spikes over his spine had already started darkening. If he made it to adulthood, he would end up about the size of a chihuahua and the dorsal spikes would be solid black. Blood oozed through a bandage on one leg.

"Dumped. Left him in a box by the door when the office was closed for lunch. No intake form, so I don't have any history." She sounded resigned. One thing we bonded over, alongside karaoke and the awful beer served at The Stag, was our belief that most people really did try their best. There were outliers, of course, but sometimes leaving a roc by the door at the county shelter was the best of a bunch of bad options.

I looked into the carrier again and gentled my voice. "Hi there, buddy." Most of the wild rocs in the country were coming in through portals in the deep south; we occasionally had one show up here, like the one I'd been examining when the newspaper photographer had snapped that picture, but this one was almost certainly a pet. Looking back up at Jeanette, I said, "I'll do my best, but don't hold your breath."

"Thanks. Do you want me to take those babies with me now, or are they okay here for a day or two?"

I looked over at the cage holding the whatsits, who were sleeping in a pile next to what was left of the ribs. Most of the bones had been chewed through. "Go ahead and leave them. They're not that much trouble now. Fred seems to know what they are, so maybe I can get some more information out of him."

"Still haven't figured out his real name?"

"Not yet. But he's really starting to feel like a Fred now."

Joey had been setting up the treatment table while we talked. I opened the carrier and gently stroked the roc's neck. Most rocs were extremely friendly, but they did have sharp teeth, and any animal could lash out if startled, especially one that was injured. The roc lifted his head and nuzzled my hand, then put his head back under his wing. I scooped him up and put him down on the table, then handed the carrier back to Jeanette. "I'll let you know how it goes."

"Okay. See you guys later." She waved as she passed Fred. "Bye, Fred." Once again, he copied the wave.

Heart sinking, I did a quick exam of the roc, leaving the injured leg for last. Other than dehydration and some mild obesity, there weren't any obvious problems. Unfortunately, I was pretty sure what I would see under the bandage. Every roc injury I'd ever seen, no matter how minor, had eventually degenerated into a huge necrotic mess. Even when I tried to clean and close the wound, the tissue was so friable that sutures pulled through. With the last one I'd taken to surgery, I'd used extra-wide margins to get back to skin that should have been completely healthy, but it was already falling apart by the time I finished. Every tissue sample I'd sent to our pathologist had been too degraded to get any useful information.

I started to unwrap the bandage and heard Fred hiss behind me. When I looked back, he was punching on the tablet. He held it up and showed me the screen. It was too far away for me to read, so I picked up my phone. "No blue," I read out loud. I frowned and shook my head a little. "I don't understand."

Fred went back to typing. "Meat red *** blue bad *** ***"

I read it aloud and looked at Joey. "Does that make any sense to you?"

"Not a bit. He certainly does seem excited about it, though."

Fred pushed his chair over to the doorway and flipped off the light switch. With the light coming in from the hallway, the room still wasn't very dark.

I rubbed my forehead where a headache was threatening to start. Joey giggled. "I don't know what's going on, but watching the two of you try to make sense of each other is making my day."

Fred typed some more. "Need red."

I looked at the lights and then back at Fred. "Joey, do we have those red Christmas lights somewhere?" I re-wrapped the part of the bandage I'd taken off. Photosensitivity might explain why healthy tissue fell apart as I worked on it. The bright lights of surgery would make the worst possible environment.

"The receptionists will know where they are. I'll ask." She cradled the roc in the crook of her arm and left the treatment area.

It took Joey ten minutes to dig out the Christmas supplies from the shed. During that time, I clipped surgical drapes onto IV stands in our tiny operating room to make a three-sided shield against light coming through the door. Joey turned off the room lights and plugged in the strand. I looked over at Fred. He gave an ambivalent thumbs-up and down gesture.

"That clears it all up, thanks." I wasn't sure I could see well enough to do surgery using cheap Christmas lights, but it was worth a try. I was tired of having tissue turn to mush in my hands. If this worked, we could figure out how to light the OR so it was less festive and more practical.

John came over to lean on the OR doorframe just after Joey and I had anesthetized the roc and switched from the overhead lights to the red LEDs, plunging the room into gloom. "Trying something new?"

I cut off the bandage as I answered. "According to Fred, we need to avoid using light in a certain spectrum. I think. Maybe." The roc's leg had four slashes, only one of which was very deep. "The translation wasn't super clear. Hey, do you have time to clean this while I scrub?"

"Sure."

Fred was still standing in the OR, though he'd left the tablet in the treatment room. I looked around and saw one of the afternoon receptionists passing by in the hallway. "Debra, can you get a mask for Fred?"

"Sure, Dr. C." She grabbed a mask out of the cupboard and gave it to the verdiran, pantomiming putting it on her face and tying it behind her head. It figured. Everybody was better at charades than I was.

I finished scrubbing and dried off. Back in the darkened OR, I closed my eyes briefly to allow them to adjust, then pulled on gloves and probed the deepest gash. I'd be able to clean up the edges and close it pretty easily as long as the tissue didn't start falling apart on me.

Clipping a scalpel blade into the holder, I got started. Working by Christmas lights was not easy. I found myself leaning closer to the patient so I could see what I was doing, to the point where I almost put my mask in the wound, a rookie surgeon's move I hadn't made in years. My suture lines looked like a drunkard had taken a stab at surgery. However, for the first time in all of my roc procedures, the tissue handled well. Maybe we could actually save this one. If this was the solution, I would learn to do surgery in the dark.

I finished up, dropped my needle into the sharps container, and stretched. "Go ahead and wake him up. I'm just going to get a bandage on that before I turn on the lights again." Joey turned off the anesthetic gas, and I grabbed supplies from a cabinet and put a light bandage over the wound.

Fred didn't object, so I flipped the overhead lights on

and unplugged the string of LEDs. I pulled off my cap and mask and stayed with Joey, waiting for the roc to wake up. The beginning and end of anesthesia were the times animals traditionally tried to die, although I hadn't seen anesthetic problems with rocs before. Usually I lost them when the wounds became necrotic and parts rotted off.

The roc climbed to his feet and wobbled a couple steps before sitting down. Joey rubbed his head. I left her to finish waiting for him to be awake enough to be left alone and grabbed my phone. "Thank you," I typed and showed the output to the verdiran. How could we not have a sign for that yet? He nodded and crutched back to the treatment room.

If Fred had just solved our roc problem, he was welcome to stay at my house forever.

LATER IN THE EVENING, Fred sat on the kitchen floor with the whatsits wobbling around beside him. Their eyes were open, but they still seemed to be exploring with their noses. Both cats were perched on the counter, staring down at them. One baby made an uncoordinated leap into another and they both fell over.

I sat down at the table and watched them for a few minutes until I remembered I needed more information and Fred might have it. I handed him the tablet.

For this, it might help to explain why I was asking questions. *"I need to find a home for the adults."* That earned me a confused head tilt, which made me wonder how my words had been translated. Investing in sign language lessons might be the most efficient thing, but he wouldn't be staying long enough for that to be really useful. *"Can they climb?"* I mimed pulling myself up a ladder.

It turned out that adult whatsits did not climb, but they did like to dig, and they could swim. Where we got stuck was his insistence that we didn't need to find some place for them to live. There was no way I could just release them. They were too dangerous. Fred tried to explain, but all I could get out of the conversation was that when the babies were bigger than half of a house cat, he would do something. The specifics of what he would do remained untranslated, even though he tried at least ten different ways. The closest we got was that he would walk with them and push them, but I still didn't understand. He promised he wouldn't kill them, but I didn't see how else he was going to keep everyone safe.

I was trying to think of a different way to come at the problem when Antonia knocked at the kitchen window. I waved for her to come inside.

"What are those adorable creatures?"

I stopped her before she could grab one. "Careful, they have very big claws. I've been calling them whatsits. Fred knows what they are, but we don't have a translation for what he calls them."

Antonia picked up my phone and looked at the app. "How clever! This would have made my trip to Spain so much easier. As it was, I spent a night in jail before we could find someone to tell them why we had borrowed the donkey."

I opened my mouth and then closed it when I couldn't think of anything to say.

Antonia handed me her phone. "How do I get that? I might need to talk to him if you're not around and he has questions."

DPAS was already worried about the diplomatic fall-out from treating the verdiran at a veterinary hospital. Having my mother-in-law in contact with him was going to send them over the edge. I grinned. Not my circus, not my monkeys.

I downloaded the app on Antonia's phone and showed her how to set up a session. Sitting at the table while Fred and Antonia watched the whatsits play and typed to each other, I thought about what Fred had been trying to convey.

If I was right, the verdirans knew how to navigate the portals to get to where they needed to go, sort of like a living database of the app Christopher had used on our hike. So maybe Fred knew what world the whatsits belonged in and could get them there.

Sending the whatsits back where they belonged would be far better than building suitable housing for them here. More importantly, if Fred could tell us the paths between worlds, everything would change. There had to be some way to figure out how to move to a specific destination, a process that DPAS hadn't figured out.

Except... Why *hadn't* DPAS figured it out yet? They'd been talking to the verdirans at the embassy for years. Was this the dangerous secret Fred refused to talk about? Why would they hide something like this?

"I have to get to book club." Antonia pushed herself to her feet. "Make sure you bring Fred over for dinner on Saturday. The poor man is going to starve to death the way you eat."

I shifted Dumbo out of my lap so I could get up. "The poor man should count his lucky stars for takeout." I hugged her and pulled a sprig of parsley from her hair. Taco liked to share her food.

Fred waved goodbye from his spot on the floor and

blocked the escape of a whatsit with his cast. He lifted his tablet. Antonia nodded and held up her phone. "Let me know if you need anything." She was already typing on her phone before she'd crossed the yard.

When I turned around, Fred was reading something that made his forehead crinkle.

I pulled out my phone and texted Antonia. *"Don't get Christopher in trouble with DPAS."*

All I got back was a laughing emoji.

12

For some reason, Wednesdays always brought the weirdest cases. Crouching at the edge of the treatment room table, I put my phone's camera in burst mode and set it off. The gremlin huddled in Fred's hands had *something* going on with her eye, but I had no idea what it was. The lens didn't have the opacity of a cataract, but it had several bright orange streaks extending from the medial to lateral edges. "There. Let's give her a break." I showed Fred the last photo as he put the gremlin back in her carrier. He shook his head.

John walked back as I scrolled through the photos, looking for the clearest one. He held out a yellow lab puppy to me, and I gave him my phone in exchange. "Have you ever seen anything like this? It's a three-year-old gremlin. Mom noticed she's running into things when she flies around the house." The puppy wriggled and licked my nose. "How come you get all the cute puppies?"

John squinted at my phone. "Because I bribe the receptionists." The real answer to that was the receptionists put the xenotics on my schedule unless the clients requested

John, so he had spots open for new puppy visits. "Nice shot. That's a new one for me."

Fred held out his hands, and I passed him the puppy. Might as well get her exposed to as many different scents and sounds as possible.

Rochelle pushed open the treatment room door. "Oh good, I have both of you here together."

John shook his head. "That's never a good start."

I frowned at her. "What do I need to bribe you with to get the new puppy appointments?"

Rochelle ignored us both. "Animal Services called..."

John touched his nose. "Not it."

Rochelle continued to ignore us. "They are out at a property where this guy has been running some sort of mail order xenotics business. Now he's gone missing, so the county is confiscating the animals. But they need help sedating two full-grown basilisks so they can be euthanized."

Keeping basilisks in California required a permit, for a good reason. A full-sized basilisk could generate an electrical charge strong enough to kill someone. Plus, they were strong and bad-tempered. Killing an animal just because it was dangerous seemed unfair, but the options were limited. Private citizens weren't allowed to own them, and zoos already had more than they needed. If animal services hadn't been involved, we might have had leeway in finding a suitable rescue home, but that course was no longer available.

Glancing at Fred, it occurred to me this could be the perfect time to test out a theory.

Even if the verdirans knew where portals went just by looking at them, that still wouldn't keep them from getting stuck if they had to sit around waiting for the right portal to appear. And it also didn't explain the regular grid of portals Christopher and I had seen on that snowy hillside.

But if the verdirans could *create* portals...

Rochelle kept going. "I know Dr. Payne usually does most of the farm calls, but it seems like it might be easier to send Dr. C out to examine the rest of the animals out there, rather than having them bring everything here."

Something about the way she said "rest of the animals" gave me pause. "How many are we talking about?" Then I held up my hand. "Never mind. I don't want to know." I thought about the afternoon appointments. "Reschedule what you can, but I don't think there's anything coming in John can't handle. I'll take Fred with me." I smiled at John. "Sorry. You might have to do something other than cuddle puppies."

He smiled back. "I have my speedy shoes on. We'll be fine here."

If the receptionists couldn't reschedule appointments, he'd be seeing patients long after the hospital normally closed, but maybe Fred and I would be back in time for me to take a few. "Okay, let me talk to the gremlin owner and I'll go."

Rochelle nodded. "I'll send the address to your phone."

Before I went back into the exam room, I gestured for Fred to follow me to the break room hall. I brought up a photo of a basilisk and then a photo of a portal, the glimmer just barely showing on the screen. I pointed at Fred, then pretended to pick up the basilisk and drop it in the portal. "*Can you?*"

Fred looked at me, clearly weighing what to say. Finally, he nodded. "*Secret.*"

This time there was no *danger* associated with the secret,

so apparently that part had something to do with the area Christopher and I had transported to.

My phone rang with an incoming call from Jeanette. She said, "I just sent you a picture of some things jumping around in the rafters. We're still trying to catch them with nets, but so far, no luck. Any idea of what they are and how to deal with them?"

I put her on speaker so I could view three blurry pictures of something that looked like a small golden retriever with the legs of a cat. "Never seen them before." I showed the screen to Fred and saw his eyes widen. "But I think my expert knows. Let me talk to him and I'll call you back." I hung up and switched over to the translation app. *"Are they dangerous?"*

Fred shook his head emphatically. Good to know.

"How do we catch them?"

He typed something that came out as a line of asterisks. He tried again. On the third try it came as *"We sing."*

If I passed that along to Jeanette, I'd never hear the end of it. I texted her, "*Not dangerous. Fred and I will be there to help catch them soon.*"

13

The drive out to the property took longer than I'd expected. Sometime during the winter, the county road I'd planned to use had washed out — I had a beast of a time turning the work truck around without getting us stuck in the mud or the irrigation ditch. Halfway through my fourteen-point turn, I realized I should have just relied on my mirrors and reversed back to the cross-roads, but by then it was easier to keep going.

Once we had backtracked and gone around the road closure, finding the site had been easy enough. Most of the farms we'd passed on the way looked deserted, but here someone had built a house with marble columns, a pool, and lion statues on plinths guarding the gate at the turnoff. It wouldn't have been out of place in the Hollywood hills; here, it just looked ridiculous.

"Hang on." I gunned the truck through the open wrought-iron gate and over the brick driveway. Jeanette had said the barn was in the back, so I ignored the curve of the drive toward the house and went straight, onto a gravel road that fit the setting more than the ostentatious house. A fallow field bordered by an irrigation ditch lined one side of the road, and closely planted olive trees crowded the other. I really hoped there was some place to turn around up ahead.

After nearly a quarter mile, I saw two large barns with an empty area in front. One barn looked old enough to have been built as part of the original farm, with a patchwork of corrugated tin covering most of the roof and rotting wood planks making up the walls. The other building was newer and bigger, made of cinder block and steel. One end was covered by a roll-up door big enough to back a truck into. There weren't any windows. Two turbine vents rotated lazily on the roof, but I saw no evidence of any air conditioning. During summer, the building would be sweltering.

Jeanette came out of the big building and waved. Fred waved back, making her smile. I pulled the truck around in an arc and parked facing the direction we'd come. *Always park so you can leave in a hurry*, John had told me when I'd first started working for him. *That way, you're also less likely to run over the farm dogs on the way out.*

The road had been recently graveled, but everywhere else was covered in mud. As I pulled on my rubber boots, I looked over at Fred's feet. The shoe we could just hose off, but the cast had to stay dry. I held up one hand like a stop sign. "Stay."

Jeanette followed me around to the side of the truck. "Does he know sit and speak too?"

"Hush, or I'll let you deal with the basilisks on your own." I pulled out disposable boot covers we used in quarantined areas and a roll of white tape. Mud sucked at my boots as I went the rest of the way around the truck and opened the passenger door. I double-bagged Fred's cast and wound tape in a tight spiral up to his knee, then put a boot cover on the good foot as well. If the cast got muddy, we'd just have to cut the plaster off when we got back to the hospital. "Where are the basilisks?"

"In the far building. Follow me."

I grabbed insulated gloves, a bright red pig board, large lawn bags, and the drug box before trudging after her, Fred sliding along on his crutches at my side. The pig board, a lightweight plastic panel I'd only used once for its actual purpose of herding swine, banged against my leg with every step. As we moved past the cinderblock building, the mud got deeper. Two-by-fours propping up the outside of the leaning barn kept it from collapsing completely. The tilt of the building combined with the mud in its path meant the door only opened about a foot.

I eyed the two-by-fours doubtfully. "This thing isn't going to fall down while we're inside, is it?"

Jeanette shrugged. "If it does, I have the fire department on speed dial."

Fred and I looked at each other. He put a hand on the building and pushed. Nothing moved. He flashed me a thumbs-up and carefully maneuvered his way through the doorway. I handed the pig board through to him. "I'm going to close the door so we don't have to chase these things around an olive grove if the drugs don't work, okay? Don't let anyone open the door." I took an involuntary step back as the structure creaked in a gust of wind. "Don't let anyone lean on it, either."

Jeanette patted my shoulder and gestured to the big building. "Yell, if you need me. I'll be right over there taking pictures."

I nodded and forced myself through the opening, dragging the door closed behind me, and securing it with a clip on a chain. At what point did it seem like a better idea to hang a chain near a door to keep it closed rather than truing up the building so the latch worked and the structure didn't collapse?

The odor of mold wafted up from the wet straw beneath my feet. I looked around in the dim light of the overhead fluorescents. Makeshift cages, some no more than wooden pallets and baling wire, were stacked on top of each other, from the floor to the ceiling all around the perimeter of the room and in rows down the center. Most of them were open, the animals within already gone, but in the back corner, Fred crouched, examining a large iron cage that might have held a tiger at a roadside attraction — back when people dragged their families along for a two-week drive and called it a vacation.

I shuffled over, a little amazed that basilisks survived in these conditions. They couldn't have been here long. No sunlight, foul air, and the cold that seeped through my boots would probably kill them within a month, but it would also irritate them in the meantime. A grumpy basilisk was not a safe basilisk. I looked down at the urine-soaked straw under my feet. My boots would insulate me as long as I kept on my feet, but if I got knocked down and the basilisk shocked me, I'd be in trouble.

Fred stood up and turned his head as if he were searching for something, eyes half-closed.

I waved to get his attention, then drew a rectangle in the air and mimed shoving something through it. "Yes or no?" I asked, nodding and then shaking my head.

He nodded. He repeated my rectangle and followed it by putting a hand on his own chest. Then he unfurled both hands at me and mimicked my shoving gesture.

Dang it. I'd been hoping he could multitask and help me herd basilisks, but it looked like I was on my own. I waved again, pointed at the cage, and made a rectangle near the gate. If we planned this right, I could just leave the cage closed and prod the basilisks through the bars. Neither one of us would risk getting singed.

Fred shook his head and wandered around the building, crutches sinking into the fetid straw. He paused near the opposite corner and started moving a stack of cages out of the way.

I trudged across the building to help him. "You know, if you're trying to make it as inconvenient as possible, we could maybe herd them through the center of town first. Create a new tradition, the first annual River Terrace Veterinarian Roast and Electrocution Parade." I heaved a roll of filthy chicken wire to the side. "Finish it off with a barbecue where we invite everyone to watch what you're doing."

He looked over at me and pointed to my phone and shrugged.

I took out my phone, ready to ask him if we could try for something a little closer to the cage, but I didn't have coverage, so the app didn't work. I shook my head. "Never mind. Not worth the trouble of translating."

By the time we had cleared the perfect spot to send basilisks back to wherever they needed to go, I was covered in sweat and a grime that came from a mixture of rust, urine, and feces. On top of it all, my feet were so cold that I could just barely feel them, which made clomping around in oversized boots on uneven footing just that much harder. In a better world, we would have been able to drag the cage with the basilisks over to the spot Fred had chosen, but with the way everything had been stacked, that would require clearing out half the building first.

We needed to get this done before anyone got curious about why it was taking so long.

I used empty crates to block off the other routes, so there was just one path to where Fred stood on a short stack of pallets. All I had to do was open the cage door, convince the basilisks to come out, somehow get behind them, and keep the pig board between us as I nudged them in the right direction. Simple, as long as I avoided being trampled, bitten, and electrocuted.

OSHA would not be happy with this plan.

Fred sat on his tower of pallets and glanced back at me, then patted the planks near him. I took a seat, wondering if I really wanted to be that close to him when he opened a portal. If it popped up in the wrong spot, I might take a quick trip to a world full of basilisks. Still, he seemed to know what he was doing, and I'd asked him to open the portal in the first place.

With the chunk of carved wood in one hand, Fred stared at the spot we'd cleared. I waited, cold seeping up through the boards until my rear end was as cold as my feet. Finally, a shimmer of light floated in the air, hard to see in the gloom of the barn. Fred leaned back and looked at it, then waved his hand and huffed a quick breath. The portal disappeared.

He scratched his head and concentrated again. I waited. Outside the building, I heard the rough idle of a heavy pickup, likely one of the animal services trucks. The building timbers swayed and creaked, and one section of the roof clanged as the wind picked up the corner and dropped it again.

It took Fred two more tries until he had a portal that satisfied him. This one came with the salty taste of the ocean. His touch on my shoulder startled me. Fred opened his hand toward the other side of the building where the basilisks waited and made a sweeping motion toward the portal.

It was my turn now.

14

I had shuffled halfway across the barn when it occurred to me that portals were bidirectional, and if Fred thought this would be a good place to send these basilisks, there were probably others in the area that might come in the other direction. I picked up the pace, trying to stomp some feeling back into my feet as I slid around on the uneven straw.

The basilisks huddled in the back corner of the cage, armor plates flattened, while I unclipped the latch on the door. "Time to go home, guys." That earned me a low growl and a crackle of electricity along the spines of the one in front. After pulling on the thick gloves, I picked up the pig board — now covered with a layer of dirty water — and held it in front of me as I leaned over and swung the cage door open. I braced myself for them to charge.

The basilisks didn't move.

"Come on." I patted the cage.

Both of them growled and shuffled back and forth in the corner.

Fred coughed. I glanced back and saw him making

shooing motions toward the portal, his forehead wrinkled in verdiran laughter.

"This isn't funny, you jerk," I called back at him. I turned to the basilisks in front of me and rocked the cage as much as I could. The animals moved a few inches, but backed up as soon as I stopped. Leaning the pig board against the cage where I could quickly pick it up again, I grabbed the bars with both hands and shook the cage. "Let's go!"

The pig board slid to the ground. The front basilisk exploded into motion, running out the door and bashing its well-armored head into the plastic shield, knocking the pig board away. I vaulted on top of the cage and watched the basilisk destroy the pig board, biting and stomping on the plastic until it was completely deformed. The second basilisk shuffled out and directed a stream of urine onto the board.

Across the barn, Fred leaned back on his elbows to watch the spectacle.

Eventually, the first basilisk got tired of attacking the board and looked around. I reached down to swing the gate closed. At least I wouldn't have to figure out how to get them out of the cage again. I just needed to move them to the portal shimmering in the distance.

The basilisks wandered a few steps toward Fred. This was my chance. If I could get to the mangled pig board and pick it up before the basilisks turned around, I could shelter behind the plastic and herd the animals in the right direction.

I waited until they were both looking the other direction, then slid down and scrambled over to the mutilated pig board. The bulky gloves made it hard to grab, and one plastic hand-hold was in pieces on the ground, but I managed to get it in front of me before the basilisks turned around. I moved forward a step.

An unholy snarl lifted the hair on the back of my neck. With spines fully erect and sparking, both basilisks crashed into the board, knocking me backward. I fought to keep the shield between us, sliding around on the wet straw until our positions were reversed and I was between the basilisks and the portal, the last place I wanted to be. My movement of the pig board wasn't fast enough and one of them got around the side and grabbed the edge in its jaws, shaking its head back and forth. I pulled back, dragging the creature with me.

When it opened its jaws to get a better grip, I pulled the board free and sprinted toward the portal, the pig board trailing behind me like a lure. The basilisks snarled and followed, attacking the moving board as it bounced across the mushy straw. Ten feet from the cage, one basilisk got a grip on the board, forcing me to stop and muscle it out of its grasp, but after that it was a clear shot to the portal. Twenty feet. Ten. Five.

Fred reached down, grabbed my upper arm, and hoisted me onto the stack of crates. One basilisk slammed into the wood, but the verdiran took the pig board from me and held it near the portal. The basilisks followed it. When the edge of the board contacted the shimmering air, Fred let go and the basilisks leapt at it. Both the basilisks and pig board went through the portal.

The portal snapped closed, leaving just the faint scent of ozone behind, quickly lost in the other odors of the barn.

Fred and I sat shoulder to shoulder on the battered pallets and stared out at the building as I caught my breath.

"Okay," I said as soon as I could talk, "that went well."

Fred nudged me and swung his arms as if he were running, then gave me a thumbs-up. His forehead wrinkled.

I pushed him off the pallets and then climbed down to find something we could use to simulate two dead basilisks.

WET STRAW and mud wrapped in an old towel and held together with a winding of twine made a reasonable substitute for a basilisk carcass, especially after it was double bagged. They weren't quite heavy enough, and anyone who got close enough to touch the bag wouldn't buy it, but as long as nobody had a reason to look, it would appear we had two humanely euthanized basilisks with us.

Next on the list was catching whatever was running around in the other building. Fred and I ducked under the rolling door. The concrete floor had been hosed down recently, but the ammonia from the stacks of cages made my eyes water. These cages had a wide variety of smaller xenotics. In addition, three large pens of fleeters milled around toward the back.

Where had all these animals come from? Even if the owner had been baiting traps all over the county, it still wouldn't explain this.

Jeanette pointed up. "If you can trap or drug those things, we can open the doors and get some fresh air in here."

Fifteen feet up, the two creatures from Jeanette's pictures huddled on the exposed metal beams, looking for all the world like a couple of miniature golden retrievers that had climbed into the rafters. I walked over to get a better look and they skittered away, claws screeching as they slid on steel. In motion, they looked more feline than canine. Small as they were, they were still big enough to do damage if their teeth were anything like a cat or dog.

Fred's face lit up when he saw them and he swung toward a ladder in the corner.

Jeanette looked at me. "We've tried going up there. They just run to the other side."

"He told me he had to sing to them." I held up my hands in surrender. "I don't know what that means either, but who am I to stop him?" Fred climbed the ladder while I held it, his cast making the aluminum rungs clang.

When he reached eye level with the animals, Fred slapped the beam twice. The two fuzzies looked over at him with curiosity, but didn't move closer. A haunting low hum reverberated through the building. It took me a moment to realize that Fred was the source. The animal in front took a hesitant step forward, then the one behind it jumped over the first and ran toward Fred, tiny teeth bared.

I heard Jeanette swear behind me, but all I could do was lean into the ladder and hope Fred didn't fall on me if he had to defend himself.

The two slammed into the verdiran simultaneously, making the ladder slip sideways a few inches. When I looked up again, both creatures were clinging to Fred's shirt and gnawing on his neck. For someone being attacked, Fred seemed remarkably calm, his humming quieter now as he scratched behind the ears of first one, then the other. He climbed down the ladder, stopping every few rungs to reassure the beasts.

When he reached the ground, I got a better look at the creatures, and at the unbroken skin on Fred's neck. My brain still tried to categorize them as miniature dogs that moved like cats. Up close, the fluffy hair was matted over prominent ribs, but both animals seemed more excited about nuzzling Fred than searching for food or water.

Humming softly, Fred detached one from his shirt and handed it to me. It hesitated briefly before clutching my shoulder and burying its face in my collarbone. I ran a hand down its back and it responded with a rumbling purr that vibrated through my entire body. From my new viewpoint, I could also see fleas crawling around under all the hair. My skin itched.

"Where did he get all these animals?" I asked Jeanette after I'd put both of the furry creatures in a carrier. With the rolling door open, the barn smelled better, but the additional light made it clear this had just been a temporary storage place before the animals were shipped out to the buyers. It wasn't a breeding facility — none of the cages held babies. Most of the animals had scars expected of creatures raised in the wild.

Jeanette shook her head. "I'd love to know. But he seems to have just disappeared. His work said he didn't show up on Monday, and nobody's seen him since."

"He had a job?" When Jeanette laughed, I tried to explain. "With that house, I figured he was a drug dealer or something. Nobody around here pays enough to build a house like that."

"He worked over at Paladin Research." She waved her arm toward the west. "They bought that big facility where the mutant plant lab used to be."

The "mutant plant lab" was the common name for the plant breeding facility run by a huge agricultural company. They made chemicals to kill weeds, then bred crops that weren't harmed by the chemicals. But while the occasional environmental protestor didn't bother them, the increased portal activity in this area had made it harder to hire plant scientists. The company had pulled up stakes and moved to Idaho a few years ago.

Something about this setup didn't make sense. If this guy pulled in a large enough salary to build that house, why would he run this side business? Even at the level of care these animals had received, it would still be a huge amount of time and effort to keep them alive. But if the side business was paying for the house, why keep the day job?

By the time I'd finished examining the xenotics and writing up treatment sheets for the animal services volunteers, the sun had dipped below the horizon. My arms ached, and I had a lump on my shin from fending off the basilisks. Even Fred had the grace to look tired.

As much as I wanted to blame the smell in the cab on the furry animals in the carrier Fred had insisted we bring with us, I was pretty sure it was coming from me. I kept the windows rolled down.

Halfway along the gravel lane back to the road, I saw headlights from another truck coming toward us. There wasn't enough room for two vehicles to pass, so I pulled my work truck over until olive branches came through the passenger window and waited. As the other truck inched by, I recognized Christopher in the driver's seat. He stopped next to me and rolled down his window.

I redirected the air vent so it stopped blowing air past me out the window. Not that I wanted to dress up to see him, but did I have to look — and smell — like I'd been rolling around in a pigsty?

After saying hello to Fred, Christopher leaned on his elbow in the open window. "Fancy meeting you here."

I gestured to the barns behind me. "We were on basilisk duty. Plus, Fred had to catch some..." Glancing at the carrier next to me, I shrugged. "I don't know what they are. How about you?"

"People got some weird readings around here, so my boss wants me to set up some monitoring equipment." He stopped talking and sniffed twice.

I narrowed my eyes. "Not a word."

His lips twitched. "You really are hard on your cars."

Keeping a straight face took effort. I flicked my fingers to dismiss him. "Try not to drive into the ditch."

He let the grin take over his face then. "Stay safe." His truck moved forward as he rolled up his window. After I'd muscled the work truck back onto the gravel lane, I saw that he'd waited to make sure I hadn't needed help. I honked briefly and drove on, ignoring the butterflies in my stomach.

A few cars were parked along the side of the paved road as we pulled out, and I saw more than one person holding a portal meter. Was *that* what Christopher had been sent to check? I'd assumed he'd meant days or weeks ago. Fred opening a portal to send the basilisks home must have created a measurable response. Hopefully, the hospital truck would afford us the same anonymity among the amateur portal enthusiasts that the police and animal services logos did. I wasn't naïve enough to believe we could hide Fred's abilities forever, but the longer it took people to put the pieces together, the better.

In the meantime, I wanted to learn more about what was going on over at Paladin Research.

15

When we got back to the hospital, everyone other than John was gone. The minute the door closed behind us, Fred opened the fuzzy animals' carrier and the little creatures jumped out and attached themselves to him, one wrapped around his left arm and the other hanging on to his neck. Fred didn't seem bothered by it. In fact, he seemed to enjoy their attention and scratched them under the chin.

John came out of the office with his duffel bag. "I see your mission was successful." He reached over to scratch one behind the ears. "They're cute little snuggle-puppies, that's for sure." He followed me outside to the truck where I pulled out the black plastic bags Fred and I had used for the basilisk "bodies". I threw the first one over my shoulder and walked over to the shed with the freezer.

John grabbed the other bag. He raised an eyebrow at the way the weight shifted. "What do you have in there?"

"A bunch of dirt wrapped in some towels."

"So... What happened to the basilisks?"

I looked around to make sure we were alone. "Fred opened a portal and sent them back where they belonged."

"Huh. Good for him." He repositioned the bag on his shoulder when it threatened to fall off. "I see the zap lizards have suddenly gotten a lot better at anchoring their nest above the security camera."

My guilty start was camouflaged by heaving the bag into the corner of the shed. "Have they? I hadn't noticed."

John laughed and tossed the other bag on top. I'd dump them in the trash someday soon. To really sell the deception, I should have put the bags in the chest freezer, but if the cremation service came before I had a chance to remove them, that would lead to all sorts of questions. Plus, depending on how the week went, we might need the space.

John locked the shed doors. "I take it we're keeping this portal opening ability a secret."

"People are already weird about verdirans."

"True. What was it like?"

"Opening the portal?" I shrugged. "Not much to see. The real fun was convincing the basilisks to go through it."

John chuckled as we walked back to the truck. "I bet."

"Do you remember when I told you about the time in vet school when they gave the small animal people a five-minute lecture on all the ways a horse could kill you and then handed someone a helmet and an artificial vagina and had her go collect the stallion?" I closed the gate. "This would have been an even stupider way to die. Fred thought it was pretty funny, though."

John picked up the remains of the pig board in two fingers. "I'm beginning to wish there was a video." Then he scratched his shoulder. "I think your snuggle-puppies have fleas."

It turned out that the snuggle-puppies not only had fleas, they had lice too. These looked nothing like human lice, but still... I collected a few to send to my parasitologist friend, and then Fred and I washed the snuggle-puppies with dish-washing liquid and combed them to remove the rest of the lice. Even after I'd changed into a clean pair of scrubs, I still itched.

We picked up pizza on the way home, the last customers before the store closed, but I went off to take a shower the minute we walked through the door. Intellectually, I knew there weren't any parasites on me — lice are nearly always species-specific — but that didn't help.

When I opened my bedroom door after scrubbing off a layer of skin and dressing in an old pair of sweats, I heard verdiran clicks and growls. Fred was talking to someone; Christopher had shown him how to use the phone, so maybe he'd called someone at the embassy. Then I heard a reply and realized the second person was also in the house.

Tamping down my desire to just stay in my bedroom until the second verdiran had left, I went out to the living room. Fred waved to me from where he stood facing another male verdiran, this one slightly older. The stranger didn't even glance at me as I walked by. I saw Dumbo hiding next to the couch and Twitter circling the two verdirans.

"Would either of you like some pizza?" I went into the kitchen and set three plates around the table. The growl of verdiran conversation didn't pause. Before I sat down, I plucked my phone from the charger and texted Christopher. "*A second verdiran is at my house right now.*" Maybe DPAS would want to know. Not that I cared about that — this just felt like a situation I didn't want to face alone.

While I couldn't understand a word either verdiran was saying, I was sure of two things. First, they knew each other. After spending two days watching Fred greet new people and following his interactions with Christopher, I could tell he was talking to someone he'd met before. Probably. It was also possible that after being around humans for days, Fred just felt comfortable with another verdiran, even if he was a stranger. I was betting on them knowing each other, though.

Second, this wasn't a pleasant "Hi, great to see you, how have you been?" conversation. The harsh gutturals of their normal speech sounded aggressive to me, but the other verdiran kept cutting Fred off, and there was no softness in his movements. More than once, Fred slapped his palm against his other hand, an emphatic *no*.

My phone buzzed. *"Be there in five."*

From my spot at the kitchen table, I could make it out the back door unhindered if things turned violent. I decided to eat. Fragrant steam rose when I opened the box. I pulled a slice onto my plate. Taco flew onto my shoulder and nibbled at the bell pepper I held for her. When Fred glanced back, I indicated the chair next to me. "Have a seat, both of you."

Fred nodded, but the other verdiran ignored me, as if I didn't exist. Or maybe I existed, but I wasn't really a person. Maybe to him I was wildlife, a thing that would never rate a name.

If humans weren't people to verdirans, then Fred had definitely named the wildlife.

Fred sat down and slid pizza onto his plate. He pointed to the other chair with his fingertips, then turned to me. Ignoring the still-talking verdiran, Fred watched me pick up the slice and take a bite. He copied my moves, then paused as if examining the taste. I'd ordered "The Kitchen Sink" —

true to its name, it had sausage, pepperoni, four vegetables, plus jalapeño slices.

Too late, I wondered if it might not have been the best choice.

Then Fred gave me a thumbs-up and held his slice up to the other verdiran. They stared at each other, not talking. Then the other verdiran turned on his heel and walked out of the house. I got up to close the door before any of the animals ran out, and saw the verdiran get into the back of a white SUV with a green logo on the door, a P and R intertwined.

I was willing to bet money that Paladin Research had this verdiran on their staff.

CHRISTOPHER ARRIVED as I was on my second slice of pizza. I opened the door and tried to look apologetic, even as I felt a smile breaking through at seeing him. "Sorry for dragging you out here. He left right after I texted you. Pizza?"

His smile felt as unplanned as mine. "Since I'm already here..."

Taco flew off with another chunk of bell pepper before we made it back to the table, but I was able to keep Twitter from running away with the rest of the pizza on my plate. "Not a chance," I told the cat, putting him back on the floor. Ears pulled back, he sharpened his claws on Fred's cast, then darted into the living room. Fred waved to Christopher and offered him a beer before going back to his texts with Antonia.

I pushed the third plate toward Christopher and opened the box lid. "Watch out for Taco."

He flipped a piece onto the plate and twisted the top off his beer. "So. A second verdiran?"

"Fred seemed to know him. They were having an argument when I got out of the shower, and then he left. I'm pretty sure the SUV he got into had a Paladin Research logo on it."

At his quizzical look, I related what Jeanette had told me about the xenotics mail order farm we'd gone to earlier in the day, and the missing owner's link to Paladin Research.

The source of the xenotics was fairly obvious now that I suspected PR had a verdiran who created portals for them. That would have allowed the missing man to collect and smuggle out animals. But to explain that to Christopher, I'd need to talk about what Fred could do.

Then again... There was no way DPAS didn't know the verdirans could open portals, not after observing them for four years. And Christopher had been with me when we'd seen the snowy hillside that Fred had deemed a dangerous secret. He deserved to know what was going on, if he hadn't already figured it out.

"The verdirans can create portals," I said.

Christopher evinced a complete lack of surprise.

"You already knew."

"I strongly suspected," he countered. "After we saw them all laid out in a grid on that hill when we were hiking... That wasn't natural."

"No. I tried to ask Fred about that place, and all I got out of him was *danger* and *secret*, and since then, he's avoided the subject." I paused to take another bite and think. "Something about it seemed to bother him, but I don't know what."

"I'll see if I can find out more." Christopher drank more beer. He linked the three of us in a translation session. "I found out how to add vocabulary words today, so things will start improving soon." He started off with a simple question. *"Who was here?"*

Fred switched over to our conversation, but his answer came back as a series of asterisks. Christopher mapped that to "Verdiran X". Then he sighed. "I'm probably screwing up the database — chances are this includes a name and a job title, and even their names are usually physical objects, but this will work for now."

Fred was still typing, making multiple attempts to enter something that would translate. *"Verdiran X finds missing group. Many years missing. Far away."*

"Kidnapped?" I suggested. "If they can navigate the portals like we think, they wouldn't be missing because of the portal storms."

Christopher shrugged. *"How many missing?"*

"Many. Road blocked."

My phone rang — the emergency clinic. "I have to take this."

Christopher nodded. "I'll keep working on it."

I moved out into the living room. "This is Dr. Cunningham."

"Hi, Nessa. This is Sarah Baxter. Sorry to bug you so late, but I was wondering if you could look at some pigamus x-rays for me."

Dr. Baxter was one of the recent hires at the clinic. Nine months after graduating, she had become comfortable with most dog and cat emergencies, but she wobbled a bit when faced with xenotics, and, like most new grads, was still uncomfortable performing surgeries aside from spays and neuters.

I logged in, looked at the x-rays, and agreed there was an obstruction. Looking at the layer of fat, I remembered my first pigamus surgery. "I can come and assist if you want."

The other doctor agreed with a speed that suggested she'd been on the verge of asking. Stepping back into the kitchen, I said, "Sorry to duck out on you, but I need to go help at the emergency clinic."

Fred didn't wait for me to type an explanation. Quickly miming sewing a suture line, he nodded and then shook his head.

I nodded. "Yes. Surgery."

But he ignored my gesture to stay seated, dragging himself to his feet on his crutches.

I brought up my phone and typed into the ongoing session. "*You stay. Sleep.*"

Fred shook his head. Then, while I was staring at him in exasperation, he pinched his nose shut and wrinkled his forehead. Christopher burst out laughing. "You want me to give you a lift?" He pointed to his chest and mimed driving. Fred nodded enthusiastically.

"It's not that bad." I pulled my keys off the clip designed to keep Taco from absconding with them. Gremlins were known for that sort of thing. "And I don't know how long this is going to take." Depending on how surgery went, I might be there for hours. "If I don't bring my car, we won't have a way to get home. Fred can't walk that far."

"I'll give you a ride home. I promise." He held up three fingers in a scout salute.

Getting used to having Christopher around felt dangerous, but I ignored my worries and shoved the leftover pizza into the refrigerator, box and all. Fred probably wasn't dying to go along because he wanted to watch the surgery; they could sit in the waiting room of the emergency clinic and talk. Maybe Fred was worried about Verdiran X coming back to argue some more. "While you're asking questions, find out why he doesn't want to stay home."

16

Most businesses in River Terrace shuttered their doors at six, but it was nearly midnight, and the parking lot of the emergency clinic was almost full. The lobby was packed, both with people and animals, mostly dogs, although I saw a few cats in carriers. At least half the clients stopped speaking to stare at Fred, and the noise level in the lobby dropped low enough to hear one woman in the corner. "He's a fifth level reiki master, and he has to do almost all his healing with his left hand because his right hand is too powerful. In fact, we do most of our sessions over the phone." I nodded to the receptionists without stopping on my way to the back. They recognized me and buzzed the door open. Fred waved and crutched after me. Christopher followed behind.

There seemed to be fairly well-controlled chaos in the back until I heard loud swearing, followed by squealing and hooves running across the linoleum floor. That was likely my patient.

The pigamus darted by us into the corner. Fred pushed the animal's rear end against the wall with his cast, handed me his crutches, crouched down, and picked him up, holding the pigamus close to his chest so the flailing legs didn't get enough momentum to hurt him.

He seemed to know what he was doing, but the last thing I needed was to have to explain to DPAS how I'd let him get injured by a pigamus in the middle of the night. I touched Fred's arm to get his attention, then picked up my leg and kicked backward like a donkey. He nodded.

Two people skidded around the corner and slowed when they saw us. I recognized one as a technician I'd worked with in the past. Her name was some sort of plant. Sage? Violet? Something like that. She had a hoof print on her reddened cheek. The other woman I'd never seen before.

I introduced myself. "I'm looking for Dr. Baxter."

The second woman came forward. "I'm Sarah. I've talked to you on the phone so many times. It's nice to actually meet you. And I think you've met Willow before." She looked over at Fred and Christopher.

I made the introductions. "This is Ranger Garcia and Fred."

"Christopher," he offered.

I tilted my head toward Fred. "Fred's visiting for a while, observing how our practice works. He wanted to come along and see how the emergency clinic handles things." That seemed as good a reason as any. "Is this Piggy?"

"Oh, uh, yeah." Sarah stopped staring at the verdiran and looked back at me. "We have a table set up over here." I took the pigamus from Fred and followed her around the corner. "He seemed pretty sleepy from the premeds until I tried to get a catheter in."

"They can be wiggly." We moved into the huge treatment room, where Fred and Christopher helped keep the pigamus on the table. With the five of us working together, we were able to get Piggy anesthetized and prepped without any more escapes. It also gave me a chance to gulp down half a cup of coffee to keep from falling asleep during surgery.

I passed Fred and Christopher off to another technician who brought up the surgery camera video feed for them in the unused isolation room while Sarah and I scrubbed in. On her way back, the tech elbowed Willow and whispered. "Dibs on that guy if he's single."

Willow nodded toward me without saying anything. I pretended not to notice.

The surgery went well, or as well as it could go when we had to make it through three inches of fat to get to the abdominal wall, leaving our gloves so greasy the instruments kept slipping from our hands. Not exactly the fastest or most graceful jejunotomy I'd ever seen, but at the end Piggy was alive and minus the toy he'd eaten.

I stayed with the tech until Piggy was back on his feet. True to pigamus form, he was out cold one second, and on his feet trying to chew the endotracheal tube the next.

Christopher found me as I was stripping off my cap and mask. "That was amazing. Though I learned more than I ever wanted to know about the innards of a pigamus."

I shoved the disposable gown into an overflowing trash bin and stretched. Sarah was shorter than I was; my neck ached from having the surgery table set lower than I needed it. "Did you get anything from Fred?"

He lowered his voice, though I doubted anyone could hear us over the buzz of clippers and laughter as two techs shaved a German Shepherd on the other side of the room. "Somewhere between thirty and eighty years ago — " He stopped when I raised one brow at the range. "Trust me, that was narrowed down. Anyhow, they lost a group of people."

"Define lost."

"They couldn't reach them anymore." He shrugged. "Fred tried to explain it, but no luck. Something about the roads being closed or maybe being too far away. Trust me, that whole time you were in there pushing guts around, I was trying to figure out what he was talking about." He paused. "I think I've gone off meat for a while."

"And you didn't even get the smells."

Christopher shook his head. "In any case, they lost a group of people, but Mr. X has figured out a plan to get them back."

I leaned against a cupboard, watching the pigamus breathe. "That's good, right?" Then I thought of Fred's response. "Why isn't that good?" At two in the morning, my ability to work through problems had deserted me.

Christopher lowered his voice even further. "Because Fred thinks the changes Mr. X has been making are the reason we've seen so many new portals lately. Whatever the guy is doing, it's destabilizing things here. Mr. X either doesn't agree or doesn't care. That's what they were arguing about."

"How does...?" I stopped and sighed. "I'm not going to understand how that all works, am I?"

A short laugh greeted my question. "If you ever do, you can explain it to me. From what little I understood, some portals are anchors, holding everything in place, sort of like cables on a bridge. Mr. X is adding more anchors to change how everything hangs together. And that might cause collapses elsewhere."

"Shit." I looked up and met his gaze. "What now?"

He shrugged. "Now I send in my report and hope someone brighter than me can come up with a solution."

We wandered into the break room, where my mug had been pushed to the back of the counter. I dumped out the cold coffee. "Did you find out why he didn't want to stay at the house this evening?"

"I never got a straight answer. Maybe he just wanted to watch a surgery?" Christopher shook his head, frustration showing in the lines around his eyes. "I really can't tell sometimes if the translation is failing, or he just doesn't want to talk about something."

"That makes two of us." I washed the mug and put it in the draining rack. "Where's Fred?"

Christopher craned his neck to look around. "I'm not sure. He went off with one of the other doctors when you were sewing things up."

We finally found our verdiran in an exam room, helping to restrain a dog with itchy skin. The owners were having a great time, recording the doctor showing the alien their dog's skin. I knocked once on the door and opened it. "Sorry to interrupt, but I need to steal Dr. Fred." I made a beckoning sign.

Fred nodded to me, then shook the other veterinarian's hand. I wondered when he had learned that. He waved to the owners, who enthusiastically waved back, scratched the dog behind the ears, and then followed me out of the room.

We walked through the buzzing waiting room and out into the chilly night. Silence permeated the air. "About your cousin..." I said, as Christopher unlocked his truck.

"Marisol could pick your car up in the morning and have it back to you by the end of the day."

I slid over to the middle of the seat and held Fred's crutches while he boosted himself up. When Christopher started the engine, we weren't immediately blasted with the odor of large cat pee, which I had to admit was a huge improvement over being in my car. "Fine." Maybe I could charge it to DPAS since Fred was the one complaining. "Thanks for driving tonight."

"Any time."

LATER THAT NIGHT, I removed the necklace holding my wedding and engagement rings, just as I did every night. When we'd first married, I'd enjoyed the symbolism of a ring on my finger. The practicality had been a different matter — I couldn't scrub in for surgery while wearing a ring. One time my rings had gone through the laundry in the pocket of my scrub pants, and another time they'd been knocked off the shelf into the wastebasket. After I'd spent a panicked hour searching through the hospital trash, I'd switched to wearing my rings on a thin gold chain around my neck.

Taco swooped down and grabbed the necklace before I could hide it in my bedside table. She burbled with delight as I chased her back out to the living room. Fred looked up from the recliner as we went by. "You know, this is why gremlins end up in the shelter," I called out, though I wasn't sure whether I was speaking to Taco or Fred. From the way Fred's brow wrinkled, he found the situation as funny as the gremlin did.

In the kitchen, I bribed Taco with a piece of broccoli and some head scratching until she let go. When she flew off to show her edible treasure to Fred, I waved to him. "Good night."

Back in my room, I looked at the rings dangling from the

chain. For a while after Mark had disappeared, just having the rings near my heart made me feel closer to him. Now... Now, it felt like a habit.

Before I could think too hard about it, I opened the dresser drawer and dropped the necklace and rings inside. They would be safe in there among my socks. I wasn't getting rid of them, just letting them stay a little farther from me.

Taco flew in again, ready to dive into another tempting space. "Not this time, sneaky girl." I pushed the drawer shut and swallowed a pang of guilt.

17

Cousin Marisol was as good as advertised — when I got in my car to go home the next evening, it was the cleanest I'd ever seen it. Somehow she'd even given it that new car smell. Fred and I braced ourselves as I put the key in the ignition. "Here goes." More new-car smell poured out the vents into the car.

I left it running and texted Christopher. "*Your cousin works miracles.*"

By the time we arrived at home, Christopher had replied. "*That's what Fred just said. Sort of.*" I looked to the side to see Fred laughing at me. "Very funny."

I considered staying and enjoying the new car smell for a while, but my phone buzzed. Another text from Christopher. "*Home yet? I have food.*"

That solved the question of what to do for dinner. I replied with a smiley face, then added a few other emojis — squid, zombie, and amphora — to keep him guessing.

I had just enough time to change into a clean t-shirt and jeans before he arrived. When I opened the door, he said,

"Someday I'll make you my famous shredded pork, but it's late and we have work to do. Ready?"

"Ready for what?"

"Fred and I are going to go by Paladin Research. You're invited, if you want to come along." He paused. "Or maybe it would be better if you stayed home, so we have someone to bail us out."

This was what I got for concentrating on my patients all day. Fred and Christopher had apparently spent the time making plans. Going *by* Paladin Research wouldn't require someone to bail the two of them out, so I assumed that was a euphemism for "breaking into". "I thought you were going to let DPAS handle it." I grabbed my phone and followed Fred out the door.

"I sent a report this morning. This afternoon I got a call from Director Noonan telling me to keep my mouth shut about this." He opened the truck, waited for us to get in, and handed me a white bag. "Burritos. They're all chicken and rice. Noonan phrased it differently, but that was the gist of it."

I showed Fred how to tear the foil away from the end in order to maintain the burrito's structural integrity. "You think DPAS is burying your report? Or are they just trying to make sure nobody finds out the verdirans can open portals?"

Christopher had the native Californian's ability to eat a gigantic burrito while driving. He headed toward the north-east end of town. "I think Immo Ring has enough money to buy any politician he wants, and DPAS is ultimately controlled by congress."

"Hang on." He'd lost me. "What does Immo Ring have to do with Paladin Research?" The Chevalier Foundation was headquartered on the opposite coast. As far as I knew, the capricious billionaire had never set foot in this county.

"Ring controls the Chevalier Foundation, and Paladin is their research organization. Ostensibly they're studying xenoplants with an eye toward growing pest-resistant crops." He glanced at me. "I assume they split off Paladin from Chevalier for tax reasons — the names basically mean the same thing, so I doubt they were really trying to hide the connection." He stopped at a light and waited for it to cycle to green.

"*That's* why Kirk Mullins was in town. Not for something in Sacramento. He was here to go to Paladin." Through the windshield, I could see fields and rutted county roads. "Okay, but what's Ring's motive for all this? He owns half the real estate on the west coast. If things get more unstable and the market bottoms out, he loses his shirt."

As far as I could tell, the only real skill Immo Ring had was making money. Whoever did his PR earned their millions. He had a habit of buying startups and claiming their inventions as his own, but as much as he wanted to pretend otherwise, advancements were made by teams, not one lone amateur.

The light turned green, and Christopher accelerated. "How much do you know about the goals of the Chevalier Foundation?"

"Something about learning to use the portals to make everyone's lives better?" I shrugged. Since I hadn't taken the job offer seriously, I hadn't looked into them much.

"Right. That's the one they talk about. They created the app I have that catalogs the portal destinations and the signaling hardware we're installing on the causeway to monitor when it's safe to drive. But they're like an onion."

He braked to steer around a huge pothole. "One of their core objectives is creating a new settlement they're calling 'Pure Paradise'. Half a million gets you and your family a spot in some pristine world, where you can hunt and fish and live the perfect life. Perfect weather. No pollution. No government to interfere because there is no government." He looked over and nodded as I frowned. "It's all tied in with a lot of white Christian supremacy nonsense, if you read between the lines."

"Sounds like a scam. Ten to one, they don't build a sewer system properly and end up with cholera." Parasitology had given me an appreciation for modern infrastructure.

"Maybe, but I think Ring is a true believer. He doesn't care how unstable everything is here as long as it stays together long enough for them to get Pure Paradise off the ground."

The open fields suddenly gave way to a manicured lawn and a complex of greenhouses, all surrounded by an eight-foot chain-link fence. Christopher slowed as we drove by. "This is it."

I craned my neck as we went past. Two large pickup trucks and a white SUV were parked near the buildings. A rolling gate blocked the entrance to the lot. No people were visible. The greenhouses looked like they'd been maintained, though from what I could see through the translucent walls, they were empty. "It's spring. We should be able to see plants in the greenhouses, right?"

"If they were doing any kind of agricultural research, yes."

But if the greenhouses were just there to hide portals... Next to me, Fred tapped the dash and pointed. Christopher stopped with the truck as far on the dirt as he could get and turned on his hazard lights; there wasn't room to pull off the road completely, and while we hadn't seen any other traffic, people often treated the county roads like their own private raceway.

We all got out of the truck. From what I could see, the fence continued all the way around the Paladin property. "As Fred's doctor, I'm advising against him climbing over a chain-link fence with a cast." Then I turned to look at Christopher, just inches away. "And as your emergency medic, I'm advising against you climbing until your shoulder is healed."

He sighed. "I didn't realize they blocked the entrance to the parking lot after hours. I thought we'd be able to get closer to the greenhouses."

Fred crutched along the side of the road in the direction we'd come from, and we followed. When he stopped after ten feet and took the block of wood from his pocket, I wasn't surprised when a portal opened up in front of him. The sweet scent of orange blossoms drifted past. I took half a step back. "Oh, no." Fred might be able to create portals on command, but what if something happened to him on the other side?

Christopher's face lit up. He pressed his keys into my hand. "If we're not back in fifteen minutes, go home. I'll call you when we're back."

Gritting my teeth, I watched the portal swallow them both. Then it winked out of existence.

Thirty seconds later, another portal opened, this time inside the fence thirty feet away. Fred and Christopher stepped out, and the portal disappeared. Fred crutched toward the nearest greenhouse fast enough that Christopher broke into a jog to keep up. He turned while running, still grinning. "Fifteen minutes."

Then they were out of sight behind the corner of the building.

I went back to the truck. Once there, I ate the rest of my burrito while I pictured all the things that could be going wrong inside the fence. Fred and Christopher might get arrested for trespassing. They could get shot by armed security. They could get pulled into a portal and Fred could trip and hit his head, trapping them there forever. This had been a terrible idea.

A truck raced by, the air wave of its passage rocking the truck I was in.

It occurred to me that verdirans might be the ultimate specialists in breaking and entering. Or rather, entering. They didn't need to break anything. Fred could get inside Fort Knox and disappear with as many gold bars as he could carry. Nobody would be able to stop him. No humans, anyhow. The verdirans presumably had some way to stop other verdirans. Or maybe not. Fred didn't seem interested in hoarding possessions — maybe that was true of all verdirans, and this was why.

If verdirans couldn't be contained in one place, that changed everything. Incarceration might be a questionable deterrent against crime in humans, but that wasn't even an option for verdirans. That probably explained why they practiced shunning — it removed the offender from society for a while.

My phone lit up with Christopher's name. "Everything okay?"

"We're fine. Fred's closing down a row of anchor portals, sort of like the ones we saw on the hike."

"How long do you think it will take?"

"Not sure. We're on the fifth greenhouse, but three of them were empty."

I turned in the seat to look back at the complex. There had to be at least twenty greenhouses. This could take a while. "If you do get caught..."

"We won't get caught." His voice was reassuring.

"Right. But if you do, act like you belong." The Chevalier Foundation's technical director's weird change in behavior at the hospital made more sense to me now. "*We* know there are two verdirans in the area, but *they* might not. I don't think Kirk Mullins could tell the difference between them. He was really thrown off when he saw Fred." And with me not knowing Fred's real name, he couldn't be sure one way or the other.

"Interesting." I heard a door open, followed by the sound of wind. Then I heard a door close, and it got quieter again. "We're in the sixth greenhouse now."

In the rearview mirror, I saw lights approaching. But instead of blowing past at high speed, the SUV came to a stop near the gate with its turn signal on. "Hey, Christopher? I think you're about to have company." After a few seconds, the SUV turned and drove into the parking lot. "Another SUV just went in."

"Might be a shift change."

A second car stopped in the road behind me. "Another car just showed up. You guys need to get out of there."

On the phone, a door opened, and then closed again. For the first time, I could hear the tension in Christopher's voice. "Nessa? Drive my truck home. Fred's making a way out for us. We'll hang out somewhere until it's safe to return. I'll call when we're back. Don't worry. We'll be fine."

The connection went dead.

"Great, just great," I muttered as I scooted behind the wheel. By the time I'd figured out how to slide the seat forward and adjusted the mirrors so I could see, a third car had entered the parking lot.

Hopefully, Christopher and Fred were relaxing on a warm sandy beach somewhere — I had my own problems. The last time I'd driven a manual transmission had been in driver's training class when I was sixteen. I still remembered the basics, but before I successfully got it into first gear, the engine stalled three times. The shift into second was accompanied by a horrible grinding noise. "Sorry, truck." The truck shimmied in response.

Then I was at the crossroads... where there was a stop sign. "Dangit." It only took two tries to get into first gear this time. "Good job, truck. We're going to be a great team." There wasn't enough room for a u-turn, so I turned left, intending to do a three-point turn, but after another three stalls trying to get the truck into reverse, I gave up. In the distance, I could see headlights coming my way. The county roads were all laid out like a grid — I could just keep going forward and turn left at the next crossroad.

I jammed it into first, winced at the grinding as I pushed it into second gear, then stalled when I couldn't get it into third. "How does he drive this thing? Sorry, truck, I'm sure it's me, not you." The car behind me pulled around, their engine racing as they roared past. I patted the dash. "Christopher will be back."

By the time I made it to my house, I had come to terms with my top speed of twenty-five miles per hour. During the day, that might have been more of a problem. At least there wasn't much traffic at night.

The local television station was holding its yearly Columbo marathon, so I settled in on the couch and tried not to imagine all the horrible things that might be happening. Columbo had just looked down at his shoes and shaken his unlit cigar when Christopher called. "Just one more thing," I said along with the actor, then muted the tv and answered the phone. "Am I bailing you out or picking you up?"

"Picking us up. But we're a ways away from where we started." He gave me the cross streets.

Unless Fred's leg had magically healed, they couldn't have run two miles, so I assumed this was some trick of the portals. "I'll be there in fifteen minutes." My car could deliver on that promise.

Fred and Christopher waved when I approached the crossroads. I pulled over and unlocked the doors. Once they'd climbed in, I did a u-turn — thank you, Civic — and headed toward home. Fred leaned back in the passenger seat and closed his eyes. I caught Christopher's eye in the rear-view mirror. "What happened?"

"We must have somehow triggered the alarm. But Fred opened a portal and we got away before they saw us. Then we went through a few more and ended up back here." He leaned forward. "Switching cars was probably a smart move." He caught my grimace and looked worried. "Is my transmission in pieces on the road somewhere?"

"Let's just say that I wasn't going to win any races in your truck."

"The clutch is a little tricky. You get used to it."

His optimism was welcome, even if misplaced. "How did you drive with one arm in a sling?" I hadn't even considered it at the end of our hike.

"Very carefully."

When I pulled up in front of my house, Christopher made a show of looking his truck over. "It *seems* like it's still in one piece." He laughed at my look and then sobered. "I'm going to go home and call my boss. With the pictures I took, I'm hoping we'll be able to create enough pressure that even Immo Ring will be forced to listen."

"Let me know if you get fired. We need someone to clean

kennels." I patted Fred's shoulder to wake him up. "We're home."

Fred blinked twice, then climbed out. He nodded at Christopher.

Christopher nodded back, then frowned in concentration. "Let me see if I can get this right." After a sharp breath, he clicked twice, growled, and ended on a grunt that sounded as if it hurt his throat. "Was that close?"

Fred clapped, but I noticed his forehead was as wrinkled as I'd ever seen it. "What did he teach you?"

"His name. Or, at least..." Christopher tilted his head and wrinkled his nose. "He *said* it was his name. For all I know, I just repeated something obscene that will get me thrown out of any polite conversation. If anyone could understand it." He shook his head. "I doubt anyone would understand me. Even I can hear the difference."

He held a hand up to one ear and waited. Fred growled and clicked.

I nodded. "Oh yeah, I can definitely hear it." I aimed for sincerity, but my pitch went up at the end, so it sounded more like a question. I hurried to speak before Christopher could call me on it. "Figure out what it means yet?"

"Not a clue. That's another task for tomorrow."

"Along with replacing your clutch," I muttered.

"What was that?" He smiled to show he'd heard me. Then he yawned. "I don't know how you do all these late nights. I need my beauty sleep. Talk to you tomorrow."

As I herded Fred into the house, I heard Christopher start his truck and drive smoothly away.

18

A few more minutes of Columbo transitioned quickly into sleeping on the couch. When my phone rang, Columbo was still looking down at his feet, but the rest of the cast had changed. According to the clock, four hours had passed.

Fred was looking at the tablet in the recliner across the room, with Twitter straddling his cast.

I groaned. I wasn't supposed to be on call. Squinting at the phone, I worked to bring the numbers into focus. It wasn't the emergency clinic, after all.

"This is Dr. Cunningham." I scrubbed at my face, trying to wake up.

"This is Maria, with Safe Bet Security. Is this Vanessa Cunningham?"

Suddenly I was awake. "Yes, it is. What's going on?" Safe Bet was the company that monitored the hospital.

"We have an interior motion detector going off at your building. Is anyone authorized to be in the building currently?"

I looked at the clock again. The janitorial staff should

have been gone for an hour, and they had the alarm codes in any case. "No." Since it was the interior alarm and not the door, it might just be a loose patient. We'd boarded a cat in the clinic once who'd been an escape artist, and I'd gotten a call every night until I'd discharged him.

"We've already notified the police about the alarm, and I'll let them know that as well. Would it be possible for you to meet the police at the building to let them in?"

"Yeah. I'll be there in ten minutes." I looked around the room again, trying to remember where I'd left my keys.

"If you get there before the police, please wait outside until they arrive."

"Sure." I hung up the phone and put my shoes back on. The advantage of falling asleep still fully dressed was that I got to save an extra couple of minutes. The disadvantage was my shirt looked like I'd slept in it. My keys were on the counter next to my backpack. Lucky for me, Taco hadn't noticed them yet.

Fred followed me out the door. I tried to indicate that he could stay behind, but he ignored me. I wondered just how often he pretended ignorance in order to get his way. Someday, I'd have to pin him down on that.

I almost took the turn to go to the emergency clinic, but remembered at the last minute that I was headed to my own hospital. The parking lot was empty when we arrived and the back door was shut. I wondered which of the patients had gotten out. We'd have to figure out some way to secure the cage better. Aside from the nuisance of having to come back in the middle of the night, false alarms irritated the police department, and they'd threatened to fine us after they were called out for the third cat incident. We kept drugs in the hospital, so the DEA and my insurance wouldn't let me turn off the alarm system altogether.

A police cruiser pulled up a few minutes later and a uniformed officer got out after speaking on his radio. "Dr. Cunningham?" He gestured toward the back door when I nodded. "I'll have you unlock the door and then wait outside while I clear the building." Fred got out of the car with me, causing the officer to do a double take, but he didn't say anything.

I put the key in the lock and turned the knob. "We have a lot of animals in there at the moment, but none of them should be dangerous even if it got out of the cage." That was the closest I could come to flat out asking him not to shoot anything moving around in the dark.

"Stay here until I come back out." He went in with one hand on his holstered gun, flashlight held in the other hand. "Police department! Anyone in here, make yourself known!" After he'd flipped on the first light switch, he slid the flashlight into a loop on his duty belt.

I heard him move around the building, calling out at intervals, then I heard a startled yelp followed by silence. He came back to the door. "How do I get these things off of me?" The snuggle-puppies were latched on to his chest and arm. "They won't let go." It turned out not to be a problem because once the creatures saw Fred, they launched themselves at him. "Are there any more of them in there?"

"Just these two. I'll get them back in their cages so we can get out of here."

The officer shook his head. "Let me finish clearing the building. I didn't get all the way through." He shook his head. "My sergeant would never have let me hear the end of it if he'd been here." He opened the door wide again. "Give me a couple of minutes. Police department!" He disappeared into the building again.

Fred transferred one snuggle-pup to me and pulled the

tablet from his satchel. He started typing, but before he could get very far, the door flew open and a large man wearing a ski mask barreled into Fred, knocking him into me. We both crashed to the ground.

Landing on the asphalt under a couple hundred pounds of verdiran knocked the wind out of me. On the way, I hit my elbow, causing sharp pains to shoot down to my wrist. By the time Fred rolled off me, the intruder was gone and the police officer took off after him on foot, yelling into his radio. I lay on the ground, listening to distant sirens, clutching my elbow and trying to breathe while Fred hovered over me. The snuggle-puppies looked down in concern from his shoulders.

"I'm fine," I wheezed, and gave him a quick thumbs-up sign to reassure him. I tapped his chest, worried he might have damaged his lungs again. "Everything okay?"

He took a deep breath and returned the thumbs-up.

Three police cars spent twenty minutes searching the area for the intruder without finding anyone. After we were cleared to enter the building, I unlocked the safe and did a quick inventory of the drugs. "Everything's here." Even the petty cash stored in the file cabinet in the reception area was still there.

An odd moan came from Fred. He frantically patted his pockets, and then hopped back to the spot where we'd been knocked down, looking behind the shed and under the bushes.

He'd been holding his tablet when we'd fallen, but it had survived with a few scratches. I took it from him. *What is missing?*

Whatever it was, he had a hard time finding words that would translate. On the fifth try, he showed me the response. *The tree.*

That answer, by itself, didn't make much sense. But I'd seen the contents of Fred's satchel the day he'd arrived, and I'd read the DPAS summary. Plus, I knew what Fred carried with him. The chunk of wood, the one the DPAS thought might have religious significance, the one I'd seen him holding when he'd opened the portal to send the basilisks away, was missing.

Suddenly, the break-in took on a whole different meaning.

This was too big for me to handle by myself. Ignoring the time, I called Christopher again.

19

By the time I dragged myself out of bed the next morning, I had texts from Christopher letting me know the verdiran embassy was involved, another telling me Director Noonan was flying out with a representative from the embassy, and a final one sent just an hour ago saying he'd come by the practice in the morning and tell me what was going on.

I poured coffee into my extra large mug (a conference freebie showing a cartoon kidney wearing glasses with the caption *The dumbest kidney is smarter than the brightest doctor*), swallowed two aspirin to make my elbow feel better, and tried not to snarl at Fred when he set a perfect Denver omelet in front of me, looking as well-rested as if he'd gotten a full night's sleep. "Next time you can go deal with the alarm company by yourself." I waved away his offer of the tablet to translate. "Never mind."

A snuggle-puppy climbed in my lap, bumping my free hand with his head until I scratched his ears. "And what are we going to do with you two escape artists today, hm?" Fred had put their carrier in the room with him when we got home, but it turned out the snuggle-pups could open both the carrier and the bedroom doors and seemed unwilling to leave anything closed. After a bit of hissing from the cats, everybody had finally settled down sometime before dawn. The second snuggle-pup was on the couch in the living room being groomed by Twitter. Dumbo was hiding under my bed.

Antonia came in while I was washing up, the snuggle-pup at the side of the sink reaching over to play in the water. She put a hand on Fred's arm as he sat at the table. "Good morning to you both." Her words ended on a laugh as the snuggle-pup launched itself across the space to land on her shoulder. "And who is this adorable creature?"

"He doesn't have a name yet." Then I glanced at Fred. "Or maybe he does have a name and I just don't know it. There's another one in the living room. They were supposed to stay at the hospital last night, but we brought them home so they wouldn't keep setting off the alarm."

Antonia raised her eyebrows, but I didn't elaborate. There was no need to worry her with news of the break-in. And I certainly wasn't going to tell her what Christopher and Fred had been up to at Paladin — she'd insist on going along if they went back, and then I'd have one more person to worry about.

MOIRA MET me at the back door when Fred and I got to the hospital. "Oh good, you have them," she said in relief when she spotted the carrier with the snuggle-pups in my hand. "I was just about to call you. Hi, Fred."

"Sorry about that." The rest of my apology was swallowed by a yawn. "I got called by the alarm company last night and I couldn't get these guys to stay put." As I spoke, I transferred them to a cage with a fresh bowl of water.

Moira grabbed a zip tie from the nearby drawer. "This ought to do it," she said as she snugged it around the latch. "It finally worked on Zimmer." She laughed. "You remember how many times that stupid cat got out while he was staying here?"

Fred reached through the bars to scratch a snuggle-pup's cheek.

I dropped my bag in the office before I remembered the other thing I needed to tell her. "Some of the verdirans from the embassy may be coming by today, so there's a chance we'll have to clear out room four when they get here. We really don't want them sitting out front." From everything I'd heard, the verdirans at the embassy would throw a fit if they were expected to cool their heels among a crowd of people in a waiting room. "Christopher's supposed to come by this morning to tell me more."

"Christopher, hm?" Moira's face was suspiciously blank when I looked at her. "How's that going?"

"How's what going? There's nothing to go." When she laughed out loud, I shook my head. "I need to check on the hospitalized patients. Don't you have work to do?"

Rochelle had a stack of messages waiting for me up front. When I warned her about the impending visit from the verdiran embassy, she nodded. "I'll get them into a room if they show up." She stretched to grab a page from the printer. "The alarm company left a message. They called you?"

"Someone broke in. As far as I could tell, nothing was taken, but if you notice something, let me know."

"Will do."

Moira met me in the treatment room, Christopher in tow. He was back in his DPAS polo shirt, jeans, and hiking boots, not what I was expecting for someone about to welcome his director and a group of status-conscious verdirans. From the bags under his eyes, he hadn't gotten any sleep at all.

Moira smiled, winked at me, and went out back to finish picking up trash in the parking lot. I led Christopher to the break room where Fred was lounging on the couch and poured him a cup of coffee. "You look like you could use this."

"Thank you." He took a big gulp and grimaced. Most people had that response to our coffee. "I spent all night on a conference call listening to fifteen people discuss the fallout of someone attacking Fred."

Rubbing my elbow, I said, "It wasn't an attack so much as him getting knocked down and robbed."

One eyebrow quirked up. "Somehow, I don't think that will make them feel better." He shrugged. "Anyhow, they're sending a delegation out here by private jet with a DPAS escort. And I've been told to get back to my field project and let them handle everything."

"Because someone robbed Fred?"

"No, I suspect it's because of the report I filed last night about what we saw at Paladin Research. Or maybe it was because I interrupted someone important to say I didn't think that chunk of wood was just a religious artifact." He took another gulp of coffee. "Don't fill that kennel cleaner job yet. I might need it."

Normally, when Christopher talked about his DPAS career, he sounded excited about working there. "Maybe you should step back for a while and let this blow over."

"No." He gazed at me for a moment, considering. Then

he seemed to come to some decision. "I told you I transferred here from Florida, right?"

"To get away from your ex and to keep your mom from
climbing ladders." I poured another cup of coffee so I didn't
have to look at him. "Was that not the truth?"

"No. It was the truth. It just wasn't the *whole* truth." He
waited until I stopped fiddling with my mug. "A friend of
mine from DPAS took a job out here with a company that's
linked to Chevalier."

"Paladin?"

"Probably, but I don't know for sure. He never told me
the name, and his family didn't know either. Anyhow, Nam
called me a few months ago and invited me to come visit
him." He frowned. "I didn't really think about it at the time,
but looking back, there was something wrong. We weren't
really 'fly across the country to go camping together'
buddies. I think he was asking for help and I missed it."

From the way he was talking, things hadn't ended well.
"What happened to him?"

"He went missing about a week later. Just disappeared."
Christopher shrugged. "All those stereotypes about DPAS
employees... in his case, they were true. Nam would absolutely go through a portal just to see where it went, and he
wasn't always as careful as he should have been. So when he
disappeared, everyone assumed he'd just been in the wrong
place at the wrong time. And maybe that's really what
happened. But that phone call... It's been nagging at me."

I watched as he carefully washed the mug and placed it
on the drying rack. "If he really did call you to ask for help,
why didn't he say something?"

"I don't know. Maybe he worried someone was watching
him. Maybe he was trying to protect me. Or maybe he just

didn't want to feel stupid." He shrugged again. "I'm not going to let this go."

Under my hand, his shoulder was warm. "I'll keep you in the loop if you do the same."

"Deal." His smile was bright despite the evidence of his sleepless night. Then he caught Fred's eye and waved. "But for now, I need to set up a grid of monitors so I don't have to take a job as your kennel cleaner."

20

A few hours later, Moira tapped on the exam room door and opened it, interrupting my explanation of diagnostic and treatment options for a gremlin with recurrent diarrhea. "Dr. C, that group you were waiting for is here in room four."

"I'll be there in a minute." When she closed the door again, I turned back to the gremlin's owner, who seemed overwhelmed by the options. Time for a recommendation. "Let's start with a fecal examination, deworming, and some fluids today. Impy will feel better with the fluids in any case. And if that doesn't solve the problem in the next day or two, we can talk about where to go from there. Sound good?"

She nodded, looking relieved. "Yes."

"Okay." I scooped the gremlin up. "I'm going to have my technicians get a sample from Impy. Then they'll deworm him and give fluids and bring him to you up front."

After I'd deposited the gremlin with Laurie, I checked my coat to make sure I was presentable and slipped into room four.

Despite the crowding, the atmosphere was frigid. Three

verdirans, two women and a man, all dressed in heavily embroidered tunics and plain leggings, stood in one corner. Fred, in cargo shorts and a worn t-shirt advertising a defunct coffee shop, leaned on his crutches on the other side of the exam table.

The DPAS contingent was crammed against the wall by the door to the reception area. Director Noonan had brought his unnamed assistant plus another two agents. Once again, the new agents weren't introduced to me. They were focused on the verdirans, not the director.

Fred was speaking to the female verdiran in the front. The embroidery on her tunic showed a series of landscapes, all connected by curling vines that went down to a tree rooted at the bottom hem.

Noonan bent slightly at the waist and cut in. "Ambassador Greenbranch, this is Dr. Vanessa Cunningham, who has been providing medical care and shelter for your colleague."

The ambassador's eyes were locked on the wall, but the verdiran man murmured in her ear as he read from the tablet resting on the exam table, where Noonan's speech scrolled by next to a translation. Multiple things became evident all at once.

First, they had a translation program that was voice activated, and seemed to work a lot faster and better than what I'd been using. Second, Noonan didn't know what Fred's real name was either — he would have used it if he had.

And finally... Ambassador Greenbranch and the other two visiting verdirans angled their bodies so they didn't look directly at Noonan, but they had no problem making eye contact with Fred. Once again, I suspected we were in "don't name the wildlife" territory.

Noonan focused his attention on me. "The ambassador

was expressing her desire for her colleague to return to the embassy with us. Perhaps you could help convince him." He spoke clearly, so I couldn't misunderstand his intent. As far as he was concerned, my job here was to tell Fred to go. As tactics went, it was a good effort. Everything was in the inflection; any literal translation would miss the implied pressure.

I shrugged off his stare. "If Fred wants to go, he can go. But I'd rather he stayed and dealt with that maniac who's opening portals for Paladin Research. And if he needs a piece of wood to make that happen, we should talk about how to get him a new one."

My words visibly rippled across the room, as first the humans froze, and then, as my words were translated, the three verdirans recoiled. Noonan's lips tightened, but that was the only sign he gave that I'd said something he didn't like. Fred stopped leaning so heavily on his crutches.

The thing missing from everyone in the room was surprise. "Oh, sorry, were we all pretending we didn't know anything about how portals are opened?" I looked at the verdiran ambassador. She gazed at the wall two feet from my head. "Four years and you thought nobody had figured it out?"

Noonan gritted out, "Dr. Cunningham, I know you have a busy schedule. Perhaps it would be best if we let you get on with your day."

I looked between him and the ambassador. "I'll leave as soon as somebody agrees to stop what's going on at Paladin. You may think he's going to create a path to the lost ones, but he's making this area increasingly unstable."

That got a reaction from the ambassador. She glared at Fred and spat out a collection of growls and clicks. I squinted at the translation. "... *natural progression which is not influenced by us.*"

Fred shook his head and slammed a palm down on the exam table. He spoke directly to the ambassador. "...*destroying this world. He anchors this world* ***..." After that, the translation subsided into a series of asterisks. Apparently, even the better version of the translation app failed when the subject got too technical.

The two human agents leaned forward. They'd been paying attention earlier, but now they were *very* interested. Neither looked at a screen — they understood the verdiran speech. I suspected I was looking at two of the people responsible for the app's existence.

When Fred stopped speaking, silence descended. Then the ambassador reached into her pocket and took out a chunk of wood similar to the one Fred had lost the night before. She slapped it down on the exam table next to him and spoke so rapidly her words had already scrolled off the screen by the time I looked at the tablet. "... *do not know who is correct.* *** *claims he will solve the puzzle. That must be the priority. You must come to an agreement.*"

And then she walked out of the room.

～

NOONAN STOPPED me before I could leave. "May I speak with you privately?"

The other two verdirans from the embassy had followed their ambassador, and the two DPAS agents had gone after them.

Fred stopped in the opposite doorway and looked back at me. I waved him on and shut the door. "Make it quick."

The director's assistant stayed. Apparently, she didn't

count. Noonan's eyes narrowed. "The next time you decide to barge into the middle of this, consider that you might be ruining four years of hard-won intelligence. Now that the verdirans are aware we know they can create portals, they'll be more cautious about what they let slip around us. This is exactly the sort of thing DPAS takes care of."

His assumption that I would automatically agree he was in charge rankled. "Then maybe DPAS shouldn't be." When he took a breath to speak, I kept going. "I don't care who gets offended. And I don't care what secrets they're keeping. There's a verdiran working for Paladin Research who is about to make this part of the world unlivable. If you can't make that stop, it won't matter what secrets you overhear."

He shook his head. "You have the word of one verdiran. Meanwhile, I have a whole embassy telling me that isn't true. Don't get fooled."

His condescension made me laugh. "You have a whole embassy of verdirans who won't look you in the eye because they don't consider you a person. Before you tell me not to get fooled, take a look at yourself."

"My sources are far more reliable than yours."

I shook my head slowly. "Are they? Or do they just have more money?" I shrugged. "I need to get back to work. The exit is that way."

BEFORE I WENT into my next appointment, I ducked back to the break room and called Christopher. "Noonan's mad that I told the ambassador we already knew verdirans could open portals," I said when he answered. From the noise in the background, he was standing near heavy traffic. "But

Fred has another portal remote control, or whatever that wood thing is."

He laughed, the sound making me wish he was here with me. "That explains the voicemail I just got from my boss."

"He didn't fire you, did he?" There was just enough coffee left in the pot for half a cup. I took a sip and grimaced at the burnt residue flavor.

"Just the opposite. I think they've decided their best chance of getting any information is from Fred. I'm supposed to spend as much time around him as I can and report all our interactions."

"That's good, right?"

"It's what I was going to do. The first part, anyway. And if I learn anything important, I'll pass it along." He paused for a noisy semi to go by. "I still have to finish up out here, so I won't be back in town until late evening. I'll get in touch with you and Fred in the morning."

"Sounds good." I nodded at Moira, who put her head around the corner and mouthed *room two*. "I have to go. Don't disappear or anything." I hung up before I could hear his reply.

21

F red and I arrived home so late the timer had already switched off the porch light, leaving the front of the house shrouded in darkness. It happened regularly, and I knew the path. I sorted through my keys by touch as I walked, listening to the squeak of Fred's crutches as he came up the path behind me.

Suddenly, a hand grabbed the back of my scrubs, throwing me sideways. I landed hard on the damp grass. My keys went flying into the bushes.

"What the hell?" I could barely see the outline of Fred where he stood on the walkway. "What was that for?" When nothing started hurting, I climbed to my feet. He held up one hand to keep me from coming any closer and looked into the shadows in front of him. Wondering what kind of animal had found shelter on my porch, I took out my phone and turned on the flashlight app.

The air shimmered in front of us, as if someone held up a thin plastic sheet that rippled in the breeze.

My mouth went dry. There was a portal in front of my door, and I had almost walked into it.

I tried to pull Fred back, but he shook me off. He crouched down, examining the edges, and clicked his tongue. He stood up and the portal vanished.

Then, as if nothing had happened, Fred walked onto the porch and waited for me to open the door.

I recognized his posture. "Really? You're just going to pretend everything's fine now?" By the time I found my keys under the lavender bush, my hands shook from the adrenaline rush. I unlocked the door and turned on every light, both inside and out, going from room to room to make sure there were no portals lurking inside the house.

A few weeks ago, I'd gotten close to multiple portals during the hike. Christopher and I had even gone *through* one intentionally to get away from the goliath chasing us. But there was a difference between seeing portals during a hike in broad daylight and a portal lurking in the darkness near my front door.

For an instant, I wanted to pack up and leave. The Chevalier Foundation would pay relocation costs if I took that offer. Maybe I'd enjoy living in Maine.

Or I could move to one of the new "paradise colonies" the foundation talked about. But... no, even now I couldn't convince myself that was anything other than a scam.

If Fred hadn't knocked me out of the way... Would I have been able to turn around and come straight back? Or would there have been some disaster waiting on the other side? Christopher told me DPAS had robots that went through unknown portals to take environmental readings and return — some of them never came back, presumably destroyed on contact with something on the far side.

"Maine winters can't be as bad as they say," I muttered as I flipped on the light in my bathroom and looked in the shower. Antonia might even like snow. I'd have to remember to ask her.

While I was busy checking out the house, Fred retrieved my backpack and went into the kitchen. The cats followed him, meowing loudly to let him know they needed new kibble or they might drop dead of starvation in the next twenty seconds. Taco had picked up on my agitation, following me around from room to room with a high-pitched commentary.

I went to the kitchen, where Fred was making up a plate of vegetables. He put it on top of the refrigerator and Taco finally settled down, chittering in delight when she found the raisins Fred had hidden under the greens.

Fred watched me pacing around the kitchen for a bit, and then picked up his tablet and switched over to our session. "*No more. Home safe.*"

I stared at him. He seemed so sure. "*How do you know?*"

"*I will watch for ***.*"

Well, that was as helpful as ever. I slumped into a chair and watched the cats eat.

Now that I had time to think about it, this portal felt *planned*, as if it had been set up specifically to trap me. Fred hadn't opened this one, which meant...

I called Christopher. If I'd been a target, he might be, too.

Once again, it sounded like I'd woken him. "What's wrong?"

"I think that verdiran that works at Paladin Research just tried to get rid of me."

22

For once, my Saturday morning schedule stayed light — when I had finished procedures during the noon break, I still had fifteen minutes to eat lunch before the afternoon appointments started. Fred had dragged a chair outside so he and the two abandoned rollers could all bask in the spring sunlight. Moira sat on the couch in the break room reading a magazine. When I came in, her eyes widened. "We left you time for lunch, Dr. C? Quick! Tell Rochelle so she can order a cake!"

I rolled my eyes and she giggled. Rochelle had been trying to alter the schedule for years, so both John and I had at least half an hour to sit down and eat, but it just never worked out. Part of it was the unpredictable nature of veterinary medicine — we needed to have enough appointments scheduled so I could pay salaries and all the other expenses that went along with running a practice. That meant my free time was the first thing to go when emergencies or unexpected treatments popped up. But most of the problem was caused by me — I found it hard to just sit down and relax while I was in the building. Plus, there was always some-thing that needed to be done.

I put the stew Antonia had left for me into the microwave and wandered back out to the treatment room, just to double check that I'd done everything I needed to. All the boxes were ticked, and the animals in cages seemed comfortable. The only thing on the board that hadn't been dealt with was one word. *Roof.*

It was in my handwriting, but it took me a moment to remember why I'd written it. Oh, right. I needed to check for zap lizard nests near the vents. And it would be good to check the roof itself while I was up there. Better to find a problem now than the next time it rained. After grabbing the key to unlock the ladder, I headed out the back door.

The rollers were sprawled on the pavement in their harnesses. Fred waved and made as if to stand, but I gestured him back down. "I just need to go up on the roof." I pointed to the ladder bolted onto the building. As Fred watched, I unlocked the metal cage blocking the first four rungs.

Like most commercial buildings in our area, the roof was almost flat, sloped just enough to avoid water pooling. Everything was dry and dusty — we hadn't had any rain in weeks, and might only get one or two more cloudbursts before summer started. Then everything would bake in the blistering heat until the end of autumn.

A flash of orange and gold near the air conditioning unit caught my eye. "I see you!" The little lizard had disappeared by the time I turned my head, but at least I knew there was a pair up here somewhere and it wasn't just the lizards above the security camera expanding their territory.

As I wandered around checking the various vents, I repeated, "If I were a zap lizard, where would I hide?" For once, all the vents were free of nesting material, though a black widow spider had set up shop in front of the air conditioner intake, its web a chaotic mess of strands with no pattern I could discern. I left her in peace — black widows wouldn't come into the building, and she wasn't harming anyone where she was.

"If I were a zap lizard..." There was really only one more place to check. At the corner of the roof, the fiber line carrying our internet came up and went to the nearest telephone pole. Occasionally, a pigeon or zap lizard would toss a few twigs near the anchor bolt on the roof and call it good — the only reason I removed them was to keep the extra organic material from covering the drain spout.

In the month or so since I'd last been on the roof, more equipment had been added. Frowning, I stared at it. Something like a black metal shoebox with tiny solar panels had been added between a cable coming out of the building and one of the thin fiber lines going to the telephone pole. Our alarm system required its own connection for reasons that had been explained to me and I had quickly forgotten — something about firewalls and the system not being secure if anyone else had access to the router. With all the different camera feeds, it made sense to put all that on a different line anyhow. I couldn't tell which fiber line was which.

Maybe the internet provider had needed to boost the signal for some reason? Was that even a thing? But why would they use something with solar panels instead of tapping into the electricity? They'd certainly never hesitated to drill extra holes in the walls and roof before. And why only one of the two lines?

The zap lizards had taken advantage of the extra support to shove a plastic straw, a deflated mylar balloon, and a pebble together and then laid three yellow eggs with red speckles. The female lizard peeked around the edge of the black box when I examined the nest. "Very cute," I told her. "Excellent work using existing materials. And this isn't the worst location in the world." She flicked out her tongue, and a spark jumped from her tail to the bolt anchoring the fiber to the roof. In heavy winds, the mylar might fly off and dump the eggs on the ground, but for a zap lizard nest, this was actually pretty impressive. Plus, it wasn't blocking any of the vents, so I was willing to leave it where it was, especially since sparks generated by zap lizards wouldn't interfere with the signal on the fiber optic cable. I could climb down from the roof and stop worrying about them. I took a step away, then stopped and turned around.

There wasn't any dust on the solar panels.

One thing I'd noticed very quickly after I moved to River Terrace was the amount of dust and pollen in the air. Surrounded on four sides by farmland, the town was awash in dirt every time the wind blew. Leave your windows open when fields were being disced, and you might come home to dirt drifts in your living room. Even on a calm day, things got dirty quickly.

These solar panels had been cleaned within the last day, maybe two if conditions had been perfect. As far as I knew, we hadn't had anyone from our ISP working on the connection in months. Any downtime was a huge pain, because credit card transactions would fail and the phones stopped working.

Was I making something out of nothing? I took pictures of the setup with my phone so I could ask Rochelle and Moira. Maybe they'd scheduled something I hadn't known about. Or maybe the security company had come out to add equipment after the break-in.

The male zap lizard ran forward and hissed at my shoe, his tiny body puffed up as much as he could manage.

"Fine. I'm leaving. You two are in charge. Keep an eye on things up here, will you?"

Then I went across the roof and down the ladder, wondering if this was how paranoia started.

23

Antonia was stowing groceries in my refrigerator when Fred and I came home from work. "Are you going to be around this evening?" I asked as I maneuvered around her to chop a plate of vegetables for Taco. "I need a babysitter."

She darted a quick glance at Fred, who was on the recliner in the living room, buried under the cats and snuggle-pups. "Are you and Christopher...?"

"Ah, no." I didn't know what the future held for me and Christopher — friends? something more? — but we needed to resolve this thing with Fred and Paladin Research before we explored our options. "I need someone to watch the snuggle-pups. Fred and Christopher and I need to go out, and the snuggle-pups are good at opening doors if they're left alone. I don't want them to wander off." I avoided the question in her eyes by looking at Fred again. "They're fun to hang out with. But if you have other plans, I can call Jeanette."

In truth, I suspected the snuggle-pups might be content as long as the cats were here. Dumbo had gotten over her snit, and I'd caught the four of them grooming each other that morning. But I didn't know how long we would be gone, and I wanted to test whether the snuggle-pups would stay put during a shorter time period before trusting them for hours.

Antonia picked up her keys. "Let me grab my costume supplies. I can glue some beads on while I catch up on the baking show." She raised her eyebrows. "And if you ever need someone to keep Fred occupied..."

I couldn't help the laughter that came out. "I'll call you, I promise."

~

THIS TIME, we took my car.

Christopher hid a smile as I firmly led the way to my beloved Civic and its automatic transmission. "There's a trick to the clutch, I promise. I'll show you the next time we're in the truck."

I smiled without saying anything. Making plans like that seemed like admitting we were on the way to an actual relationship, one that involved driving each other's cars. Part of me — a large part, I had to admit — wanted that. But another part of me wondered if it was too easy, if I was falling into a relationship because of everyone's expectations. I was a person who had been married, so of course I would never want to be single again.

Letting myself drift had been my way of dealing with everything for the last four years. If I was going to move forward, I needed to figure out what I wanted and make my own decisions.

On the drive out to Paladin Research, we went over the plan. Mostly, it was the same thing we'd done before — I would drop them off and wait for Christopher's call to pick them up again. The only thing different was the drop-off location. Instead of taking a chance on someone noticing my car parked near the facility, I would drop them off where I'd picked them up last time. Fred and Christopher would reverse their path.

"This time we're going to avoid opening the greenhouse doors," Christopher told me. "I think that's what must have set off the alarms last time."

I caught his eye in the rearview mirror. "For all we know, they have laser beam detectors like they do in all the spy movies."

He didn't look concerned. "If anyone shows up, we'll just leave like we did last time. That's the beauty of Fred being the only one who can open portals."

Not the only one, I wanted to remind him. There was another verdiran who worked there, who was deliberately opening portals that anchored our earth to places we shouldn't be able to reach, who had made the area so unstable the federal government was talking about providing disaster relief so everyone had the funds to move away. But we had almost reached the drop off spot, and Christopher already knew about Mr. X.

I pulled off the road at the intersection. Years ago, this corner had been a place to buy strawberries and cherries during the summer, the hard packed dirt lot just large enough for a few cars to park, for the drivers to pay cash for juicy berries that had never been refrigerated and then get in their cars and drive home again. It had to have been a miserable job for the people stuck selling the produce, with no shelter from the sun and no one to take over for breaks. The whole thing had probably been illegal, exploiting people who couldn't complain. And yet... those strawberries had been better than anything you could get in the store. Now the dirt was slowly being reclaimed by weeds, but years of cars compacting the soil had taken their toll.

Fred and Christopher climbed out, Fred's crutches finding easy purchase on the barren soil. I got out and stood next to Christopher as Fred searched the area, scanning for the perfect spot in the same way he'd looked around in the barn with the basilisks. "At some point we're going to have to do something about the other verdiran," I said.

"X," he said. Then he frowned. "We need to find a better name for him. I refuse to make him sound like a bad Bond villain."

"Call him Xavier," I suggested.

"Great. Now he sounds like he belongs in a BBC drama."

That made me laugh. "Call him what you want. We still need to find a way to stop him. If Fred closes anchor portals and Xavier just opens them again, we'll be stuck in this cycle forever."

"Yes, but this should buy us a little breathing room. Fred said the first portals tying everything together would have taken weeks to form. Each one after that gets a little easier. The more portals Fred closes, the longer it will take Xavier to recreate them. And in the meantime..."

Fred pulled the chunk of wood out of his pocket and concentrated. A band of light shimmered into being.

"In the meantime..." I prompted.

"Fred thinks he can help Xavier find another way to get to the lost ones. A path that won't tear our earth apart." He reached out a hand and almost touched my shoulder, but his arm dropped as Fred beckoned. "That's my cue."

"Be careful."

He grinned, half his attention on the portal. "Always."

Then he and Fred gave identical waves and stepped forward. Their outlines lit up, and they were gone.

I kicked at goat's head thorns on my way back to my car. For now, my job was to wait. I could go home, but there was always the possibility they'd have to leave as soon as they made it inside Paladin. I'd wait a while just in case they needed a quick retrieval.

My phone rang. The number wasn't one I had saved in my contacts, which meant it was someone from the emergency clinic. "This is Dr. Cunningham," I answered.

I didn't recognize the deep male voice on the other end. "This is Simon from Safe Bet Security."

My heart sank. "Not again."

"Sorry?" Before I could answer, he spoke. "I'm calling about the photo you sent in today. I finally got the time to go check out the setup on your roof."

"Ah." I hadn't sent the photo to the security company, but presumably Moira or Rochelle had. "And?"

He paused, then spoke slowly, as if trying to figure out the best way to phrase his question. "Is anyone from your hospital having problems with a stalker? A jealous spouse, maybe? Probably someone with access to a lot of money, or maybe government connections."

When I didn't answer right away, he continued. "That device you found connected to our fiber line is sending a copy of all the camera feeds out on wifi and delaying the signal to our office by fifteen minutes. Or it was — I disconnected it. But I had to contact a buddy who worked at the NSA to find out what this thing is. It's not the sort of thing someone can buy for a few bucks online."

As far as I knew, none of my employees had a stalker. But all sorts of people were interested in Fred. Every room inside the hospital aside from the restrooms had at least one camera, plus there were the exterior views. Presumably the DPAS would have access to this sort of spyware. But so would the Chevalier Foundation and all of its subsidiaries. Immo Ring had enough money to purchase a small country; buying some high-tech gadget would be nothing. There was a good chance he owned the company that made it.

Toeing the dirt, I tried to figure out what to do next. "It's removed now, right? Is there any way to make sure another one doesn't get installed?"

"We can add visibility to your roof," he answered, doubt in his voice. "Another two cameras would take care of it, but you'd have to bump up your coverage level to get someone to constantly monitor the feed." He let out a breath. "It might be more effective to just go on the roof every once in a while and check."

Somehow I doubted he was supposed to tell me that instead of convincing me to spend more money. "I'll start with that while I think about it. Thanks for letting me know."

"You're welcome. I'll give you a call if my buddy has any way of tracking down the owner of this thing. Mind if I keep it?"

"It's all yours." I hung up and shoved my phone back in my pocket. Someone else having access to all the camera feeds was a little creepy, but it wasn't like we all didn't know everything was being recorded anyhow. Nobody looked at the feeds unless something was stolen or someone was assaulted, both of which had happened on rare occasions.

The fifteen-minute delay bothered me more. It meant anyone who broke in had a quarter of an hour before the alarm company was even notified. That worried me.

I was still thinking about it when a white SUV pulled off the road onto the dirt lot, stopping just in front of my Civic.

Stupidly, my first thought was they'd been confused by my presence and thought the fresh berries were back. Then I saw the Paladin Research logo on the door and my stomach dropped. A truck pulled in behind my car, boxing me in.

Kirk Mullins stepped out from the passenger seat in the SUV, his suit as fresh and crisply pressed as it had been when he'd come by the hospital. "Dr. Cunningham! We thought we might find you out here."

A huge man in tactical gear walked up to me, and I hit the side of my car when I flinched away.

Mullins shook his head. "Give Billy your keys. He's going to take care of your car." He gestured to the SUV. "Come along. We need to talk."

We were miles from town. Nobody else was around. There was no point in running on foot. I let Billy take the keys from my hand.

The inside of Mullins's SUV smelled new, the upholstery so clean it might have just come off the lot. It was also spacious, but I had to fight off a wave of claustrophobia as two large men sat down in the adjoining seats. The wheels threw up a cloud of dirt as we jolted back onto the asphalt of the county road.

It took almost as long for the gate to roll open at Paladin Research as it had for us to drive there. The SUV pulled into a spot close to the administration building. Billy and my Civic were nowhere to be seen. I stood next to the SUV and watched the gate roll closed again. My Civic hadn't been brought here, I realized, because I wouldn't be driving away.

My fingers tingled from the cold that knifed through me.

"This way, Dr. Cunningham," Mullins called as he walked around the building, heading for a row of greenhouses. When I didn't immediately move, the two men in black khakis bracketed me and took my upper arms. When I pulled back, they kept moving forward and my feet were lifted off the ground for the next six feet, like I was a small child between two adults. In an action movie, I would have stolen their guns and run away, but in reality, any attempt at resistance would likely end with a mouthful of dirt and a spiral fracture of the humerus. When my feet were back on the ground, I walked forward.

We headed along a concrete sidewalk, past sun-faded signs that numbered greenhouses and exhorted users to change shoe covers and lab coats upon entering a new section. At building seven, Kirk Mullins held open the door. "We'll wait in here."

Christopher had shown me the pictures he'd taken the last time he'd been here, so I knew what to expect. It was still odd to walk into a large building meant to grow plants and see a neat grid of portals, all billowing in non-existent breezes. In the closed environment, the ozone tang sizzled in my nostrils. I also got hints of loam, and sea salt, and... vanilla? Something like vanilla, anyhow, though it was a smell I'd never encountered before.

From the closest portal, a small black rodent appeared. It sniffed, whiskers twitching, and then darted to the edge of the greenhouse and ran from us. I saw a glow as it transported away. When I looked around, I noticed all the different cobwebs and birds nesting on the building frame. Plants I didn't recognize sprouted from the gravel near the edges. An insect screamed rhythmically in the shadows.

These rows of portals might be destabilizing my world, but I was pretty sure they were changing the ecosystems of other places as well. The other grid Christopher and I had seen during our hike was on a barren snowy slope, and the portals had been spaced farther apart. Here, everything that came out of one spot would be trapped until it went elsewhere.

"Fine," I said, crossing my arms. "I'm here. What do you want?"

Mullins regarded me with a disappointed look, the lighting of the greenhouse making him look more like a medieval monk than ever. "It didn't have to be this way, you know. My employment offer was entirely sincere. You would have signed an NDA and that would have solved all our problems. Then Chevalier would have gained a mind capable of addressing some of our xenofauna challenges, and you would have had a chance to earn a spot in Pure Paradise when it opened."

So much about that didn't make sense. I latched onto the first statement. "Why would I need to sign a non-disclosure agreement?"

Mullins cocked his head. "Our navigator swore you saw him removing the old tethers. Was he mistaken?" He huffed a breath halfway between a laugh and a derisive snort. "All that effort for nothing." Then he frowned. "But, no. Why else would the other one be here? You had to have sought him out for a reason."

A spider the size of my fist abseiled from the beam just above his head. Mullins saw me staring at it and glanced up. He stepped to the side and pulled out his phone. "Rory, have them spray building seven again tomorrow morning, and make sure that gets added to the weekly schedule." He hung up so fast, there couldn't have been time for the other person to respond.

My brain buzzed, trying to make sense of what he'd said. Assuming his "navigator" was the verdiran we'd been calling Xavier, and "tethers" were the same thing as anchors, he was talking about what Christopher and I had seen during the hike a few weeks ago... which had been right before I'd received the first offer from the Chevalier Foundation.

Just before I'd returned through the portal to our world, I thought I'd seen another verdiran. Had that been Xavier? I'd only caught a glimpse of him. Fred had looked at my drawing. *Danger. Secret.* But he hadn't told me the source of the danger, or why it was a secret. Was the place forbidden? If Xavier had been changing anchors in secret, he must have panicked when he saw me. If I'd told someone what I'd seen, he would have been in trouble.

Except I hadn't known what I needed to tell them.

Fred had known. But Fred wanted to help Xavier find the lost ones safely, not get him censured.

I had a feeling *this* information would get the ambassador involved... if I could stay alive long enough to tell her about it.

Letting my hands drop to my sides, I said, "I still have no idea what you're talking about. And I didn't seek Fred out — he got hit by a car and the human hospital wouldn't take him, so they brought him to me."

Disbelief carved deep lines in Mullins's face, but it wasn't aimed at me. "They... They sent a verdiran to a *veterinarian*? That's absurd."

I was both vindicated and offended. "Absolutely. But that's what happened. So this is all just a big mistake, and if you can bring my car here, I'll leave and we can forget all about this."

I had zero expectations my suggestion would work, but it was worth a try.

Mullins sighed. "Dr. Cunningham, I've seen the reports Ranger Garcia has filed. I can't have the two of you running around talking about this, much less helping a different navigator undo nine months of work."

So he had a source in DPAS. That shouldn't have been a surprise. Christopher had assumed Immo Ring's money controlled the department. I just hadn't realized how much access they had. They probably saw everything we typed into the translation app — that explained how they'd been waiting to scoop me up this evening.

"So now what?"

He glanced at the expensive-looking watch on his wrist. "Now, we wait for your friends to arrive. Shouldn't be too long."

Looking around at the room, I shook my head. "Do you have a chair or anything? We could be waiting awhile. And who knows what kind of venomous insects are scuttling around on the floor." That made the guard nearest the door twitch. Never fails — there's always at least one entomophobe in every group. I filed that away. Maybe I could throw a bug at him and make my escape.

Mullins's phone buzzed. He glanced at it and smiled. "It won't be too long now. They're here. They should see the posters with your picture on them fairly soon."

As much as I was hoping he wouldn't be, Mullins was right. Less than ten minutes later, Christopher opened the door to the greenhouse and walked in, Fred crutching along behind him. The guards moved forward and patted Fred down until they'd removed his portal device. Ignoring Mullins, Christopher crossed to stand in front of me. "You okay?"

"I'm fine." Now that I wasn't alone, I had a harder time keeping a brave front. I kept my voice low and tried to keep it steady. "We're screwed."

"Maybe not," he murmured. "I sent a text to my boss a few minutes ago. At least someone knows we're here."

That might have been more encouraging if Christopher

hadn't been the only DPAS employee stationed in the region. Still, it was better than any plan I'd come up with.

Mullins's phone buzzed again. He stood up straighter as he answered. "Director Noonan! How are you this evening?" He listened, then nodded. "Yes, all three are here. We'll be going out of range soon." He listened again. "Of course. Have a good evening."

"Well, shit." Christopher's shoulders drooped. He moved to stand next to me, his arm brushing against mine. "So much for that."

Fred noticed our disappointment. He shrugged, another movement he'd picked up. Of the three of us, he seemed the least worried. Of course, he was also the only one who had a good chance of making it back if Mullins sent us to a random destination.

Then he saw a portal marked with a red metal bar on the dirt in front of it and froze.

Mullins followed Fred's gaze and rolled his eyes. "Here we go again. For a race that's holding the keys to instantaneous interstellar travel, the verdirans are superstitious reactionaries." He looked back at me. "That's the other reason for the NDA. We had to swear up and down we wouldn't let anyone go through certain portals or talk about them anywhere that could get back to the other verdirans. Our navigator almost wouldn't set them up, but apparently they're necessary for what we're doing."

Necessary for what Xavier was doing, maybe. I wasn't convinced Xavier's goals lined up with the Chevalier Foundation's, though Mullins might not have realized that. "What's the big mystery?" *Danger. Secret.* This had to be related.

"If you ask the verdirans, it's because it's the home of the central tree. You've seen those blocks of wood they carry around. If you believe them, the wood has some magic they need to create new portals."

I remembered Fred's reaction when his had been stolen. Whatever its purpose, the need to have it had been real.

Mullins must have seen my doubt. "They can open the portals just fine without it. The problem is finding the right destination. As far as we can tell, the wood just works as a sort of tuning fork, so they have the right starting frequency to navigate." He shrugged. "It's too bad, really. We were hoping we'd be able to cut out the middleman as soon as we engineered our own version of the central wood, but it looks like it's going to take a while longer."

Christopher shifted. "And now that we know about those portals you weren't supposed to let anyone see?"

Mullins waved that away. "Relax. We're not murderers. Once everything is done, you'll be released unharmed. And the verdirans don't kill people either, at least not directly. The worst they would do to another verdiran is shun them. You and I they might just abandon somewhere to keep their precious secret safe. We can't open portals, you know, so they don't consider us even worth punishing."

He pocketed his phone. "Now let's go take the tour."

24

G oing through a portal would never *not* be weird, but at least now I knew what to expect. We lined up in front of a silver plaque on the ground labeled "Gamma 47". A guard went through first, and then we all moved forward. Just before we touched the shimmering air, Christopher and I reached out to each other. His hand was warm and calloused. I focused on that as my skin tingled and everything went dark.

The transition took just a couple of seconds. We emerged in an emerald green field in the mid-day sun.

Mullins gestured broadly with one arm, as if showing off his own creation. "Welcome to Pure Paradise."

Rolling hills surrounded us. When I looked past Christopher, I saw an impossibly blue lake. In front of us, a concrete path curved toward the water and then wound around the shore, with offshoots going to glass and granite houses in the hills. I squinted in the sunlight and counted. Either paradise was only meant for about ten families, or there was a lot we weren't seeing.

Fred looked confused.

Christopher dropped my hand and knelt, running his hand through the blades of grass. "This is Kentucky bluegrass."

"Lovely, isn't it?" Mullins strode toward two golf carts.

We followed. The breeze changed direction, giving us hints of algae and... weed killer? Now I had a pretty good idea of what was on the other side of the hills. "So... You picked a spot, wiped out all the native plants and animals and seeded it with grass? Holy shit, that's..."

"It's a thing of beauty."

Christopher shook his head slightly. I swallowed my words and looked at the still water of the lake. Had they drilled wells as a source of water? Or were they using the lake? If it was the latter, the wrong type of algae bloom could kill them all. Superficially beautiful, "paradise" might be on the edge of collapse.

Christopher had thoughts along the same lines. He whispered, "I saw a lot of things like this in Florida. Throw up a bunch of condos and sell them before the land washes out underneath them."

"The whole thing is a scam," I muttered. "You can't just wipe out all the flora, sow one kind of grass, and not expect the native plants to grow back." I looked at the hills and the lake. I didn't see a water treatment facility. "And if they aren't careful about how they handle things, cholera is *definitely* a possibility."

The two guards drove us toward a cluster of buildings near the lake while Mullins pointed out the amenities — solar panels on every roof, a waterfront restaurant, hiking trails. His voice warmed as he spoke. "Plus, we're building a state-of-the-art hospital. And then there are the extras."

We pulled up in front of a building that could have been a warehouse. Fred stiffened, and I caught him checking his empty pocket. So it wasn't a surprise when we went inside to find a cavernous space with another grid of portals. I counted four military-looking types watching from the periphery with semi-automatic rifles slung over their shoulders. Mullins checked a handwritten schedule on a whiteboard mounted on the wall. "Shouldn't be too long."

The guns made me nervous. "What is this place?"

"One of the extras I was talking about." Mullins pointed at the nearest portal. "Want to hunt a sabertooth tiger? Dinosaurs that never went extinct?" His finger moved to the one beyond that. "How about an elephant? Without having to get a permit or deal with protestors." He smiled. "This place really is paradise. We can bag an elk and make it back for dinner without having to drive anywhere. The restaurant here has the freshest meat you'll find anywhere."

Now the guns made sense. There was nothing to stop the animals from coming through the portals in this direction. A sabertooth tiger roaming the hills of paradise might scare off the investors. The walls of the building were cinderblock — would that stop a bullet? Covering my mouth with one hand, I whispered, "This is like the time-share presentation from hell."

Christopher was more direct. "Why are we here?"

Mullins shrugged. "The two of you?" He indicated Christopher and me. "You have skills we could use, but you're really here to make sure *he* cooperates. Our navigator has run into some... technical challenges, and he could use a consultant."

Fred took a step forward, facing a portal two thirds of the way down the warehouse. Rubbing his ear as if he heard a discordant frequency, he shook his head. If he hadn't moved, I would never have noticed, but now that he'd brought my attention to it, I saw how the portal rippled more than the others. Ozone burned my nostrils.

An electrical arc crackled from the portal to the exposed ceiling beam. Then another. And a third. The portal disappeared, leaving behind a charred stain on the concrete floor.

I shoved my hands in my pockets. "Hope nobody was off hunting a sabertooth tiger in that one, because they aren't coming back to paradise any time soon."

Mullins shot me a venomous look. "As I said, we've had some technical challenges."

A portal near the back of the room glowed white, and the guards unslung their guns. Then a verdiran — Xavier — appeared, followed by another six men, equally well-armed. The guards on the perimeter relaxed.

Xavier ignored all the humans in a move I was beginning to accept as the verdiran standard. Only Fred was deemed worthy of notice.

And Fred was pissed.

I thought he'd been angry when Xavier had come to my house, but this was a whole new level. When Xavier came within range, Fred lifted one crutch and whacked the other verdiran in the head. Xavier fell to the ground in a crouch, hand to his cheek.

The men following Xavier ran forward to separate the two, guns aimed at Fred.

Mullins's voice cut through the chaos. "Put your guns away! Right now!"

Christopher and I had been forgotten. He edged behind me so he could speak near my ear. "If they harm Fred, none of the verdirans will talk to them again."

I wondered how far that ban would extend. The man who fired the bullet? Everyone in the room? The entire group behind this nightmare of a place? Looking at Mullins's face, I thought he also wasn't sure.

All the guns were lowered, but the men kept a protective ring around Xavier. Mullins strode forward and held up a sheet of paper for Fred to read. Right. Back to paper again, because without cellular coverage, the translation app wouldn't work. Mullins looked over at us. "As long as your friend here cooperates, the two of you will remain unharmed. But if he refuses, things could get a little rough."

Fred ripped the paper from Mullins's hand and tossed it on the floor. But when he looked at us, I sensed hopelessness. I shrugged. "Do what you need to do." Without the translation app, he wouldn't understand my words, but I suspected he would get my meaning. Fred wouldn't help destabilize our earth, not even to protect us. That much I knew. Lifting my chin, I gave him a thumbs-up.

Mullins spoke to the guards we'd come here with. "Stash these two in the distillery." He looked at me. "You'd better hope your navigator cooperates."

25

The "distillery" turned out to be a portal encased in a metal cage at the back of the room. I'd figured it out before the guard finished unlocking the gate. We'd be stuck on the other side of the portal — anyone coming back would have just enough room to stand on this side to unlock the cage.

They'd already been prepared to keep prisoners.

I pushed back against the hand shoving me forward. "Is there drinking water on the other side?" The hand pushed harder and I threw up my arm to shield my face. My fingers tingled where I touched the shimmering surface. Then everything was dark and still as I fell through space.

I landed knee-deep in snow, a star-filled night sky above me. Green lights swirled on the horizon, reflecting off a cluster of small translucent geodesic domes twenty feet away. Entranced by the northern lights in the sky above me, I forgot to move. Christopher crashed into me as he came out of the portal, and we went down in a tangle of limbs. Snow slid down my back.

I shivered as I climbed to my feet. "I think I should start

bringing a parka with me everywhere I go." In jeans and a t-shirt, I wasn't any more prepared to encounter cold weather this time than I had been during our hike.

"At least there aren't any snakes." He brushed snow off my shoulder, then moved ahead to break a trail through the snow toward the nearest dome. Between the dome's dark interior and the lack of footsteps in the pristine snow, the area didn't look inhabited, but at least we'd have shelter.

"No snakes that we know of," I said, and crunched along after him.

The door to the dome was ajar, snow spilling through the gap, and the interior was as frigid as the outdoors. Crushed cigarette butts littered the ground, as if someone had stayed in the protection of the dome and leaned through the gap to smoke. Inside, the lingering odor of ammonia reminded me of every cat spay and neuter clinic I'd ever participated in. Christopher kicked the snow out of the way and pulled the door closed. His nose wrinkled. "Smells like your car."

"It's not the air filter here, either." The translucent glass panes blurred the moving lights in the sky. Using my phone's flashlight, I illuminated the interior. From the rumpled sleeping bag and box of empty MRE pouches, someone had spent a lot of time here, but the air had a stale quality that said the building had been vacant for a while. A tiny space heater lay next to the sleeping bag, plugged into the only visible outlet. Next to that was a hot plate with an empty two-quart pot.

Opposite the door, a tunnel extended toward the neighboring dome, the entrance covered by clear plastic flaps like a supermarket refrigerator. By unspoken agreement, we headed in that direction. I rubbed my arms. "Maybe we'll find the snakes in the next one."

"Very funny." Christopher pushed through the plastic at the end of the short tunnel. The smell was stronger here. We moved into a dome nearly identical to the first, except without the sleeping bag. Open boxes lined the curve of the walls.

In the middle of the floor lay distillation equipment, the glass condenser still positioned over a receiver flask. A half-empty box of tiny vials with screw top lids lay within easy reach. The pot for boiling the original substance had a dusty film of leaves on the bottom and sides, as if someone had just dumped the contents without cleaning it afterward. I started to look more closely, then pulled back as the smell hit me. This was the source of the stench permeating the domes. "Why would anyone want to concentrate *that*?"

"And why would they need to do it in the middle of nowhere?" Christopher added.

Leaving the distillation setup where it was, I sorted through a few boxes to read the labels. MREs, toilet paper, paper towels, hand soap. They all had manufacturer's addresses in the US. Since I didn't know how many people had stayed here, I couldn't tell how long it had all been in use. If it had just been one person, they had lived here for months.

The final two domes were larger, filled with rows of waist-high shrubs, all dead. Seen in the illumination of the northern lights and the glow from my phone, it gave me the creeps. I edged closer to Christopher. "Of all the places to set up a greenhouse, why here?"

Christopher sounded equally uncertain. "Isolation, maybe?" He leaned over to look more closely at the brown leaves. "Do you know what kind of plant this is?"

"No." Though that didn't mean anything. "Antonia's the gardener." I could identify a handful of poisonous plants that would kill livestock, and Mark had taught me the names of the more common flora along the trails where we hiked, but I was no expert.

Christopher knocked away some brittle leaves to get a closer look at the stem. "It looks like something's been cut from the top here. I think this was what they were cooking out there."

This didn't look anything like the marijuana plants Antonia grew in the raised bed nearest her cottage, and I was pretty sure poppies flowered lower to the ground. "It's not any contraband I'm familiar with. My guess would be it's some sort of xenoplant they didn't want to risk growing elsewhere, but..."

"Yeah." Christopher stood up. "I guess we can add that to the bottom of the list of questions. We have more important things to worry about."

We headed back to the first dome, where the air was the freshest. The space heater moaned a little when I turned it on, then went silent.

"The solar panels might be covered by snow." Christopher didn't move. "I'll check when it's light outside."

"Assuming it *gets* light outside." The eerie green swirl was visible through the panes of the dome. "If that's the aurora borealis, and we're far enough north to see it..." Then I realized I might be making false assumptions. Did they even have the same phenomena on other planets? "What causes northern lights?"

"Something to do with magnetic poles and sunspots? I don't know." Christopher moved a stack of boxes into the center of the dome. "Have a seat. The cardboard will insulate us from the ground."

I sat gingerly, but the nested boxes were solid. Christopher perched on the stack next to me and pulled the sleeping bag around us. His shoulder warmed mine. It made me realize how long it had been since I'd just sat with another person like this.

The dome became oppressively silent.

"I almost called," I blurted. "The week after the hike."

He slowly turned his head to look at me. "But you decided not to."

"No. I kept putting it off because it just felt..." I trailed off.

"Because of Mark."

Somehow, I hadn't expected him to remember my husband's name. "I know he's not coming back. Not after all this time. But I still kind of panicked."

He bumped against me companionably. "It's okay. I get it."

"And then Antonia told me I was being an idiot."

Christopher dropped his chin to his chest and laughed softly. "Your mother-in-law is an interesting person." He raised his head and watched the lights playing over the dome. "Is that why you stopped wearing the necklace with your rings on it?"

It was automatic to touch my sternum, where my wedding and engagement rings had been for so many years. Now it felt unexpectedly smooth. "You noticed." I let my hand drop. "It seemed like it was time."

"Ah."

Only I would be stupid enough to start a conversation like this when literally trapped in a small space with no escape. I cleared my throat. "Anyhow, I just... When we get back..." *If* we got back. "I'll call. If I haven't left it too late." My cheeks burned, and I wondered if it would be any more awkward if I pulled the sleeping bag over my head and pretended to be dead for the next hour or two.

Christopher leaned against my shoulder a bit harder. "That would be good."

We watched the lights some more.

I gazed absently through the panes toward the ground. "That portal is probably our only way out of here. Unless we're actually somewhere in northern Canada."

Christopher shook his head. "Not with those constellations. Though I guess we could be somewhere in the Southern Hemisphere. I don't think I'd recognize the stars there."

"I'm pretty sure we're not in Antarctica."

He nodded. "Yeah, the portal's probably our only way out. I don't suppose you know how to pick a lock?"

"Sorry. My life of crime began and ended with ditching school once in the eighth grade."

Christopher laughed and turned to look at me. "I wouldn't have pegged you for the truant type, Dr. Cunningham. Were you avoiding class, or was there something better to do?"

"It was a stupid dare. I went home and read a book." The school had called my father, and he'd come home from work early to find me sitting on the couch with a plate of brownies. He'd tried to give me a stern lecture, but his heart wasn't in it. I suspect he was just relieved that was the extent of my rebellion.

"Okay, that part I can believe."

"Let me guess. You were one of the popular kids, maybe on the football team?"

"Soccer and track, not football. And I was too busy with workouts and homework to get into trouble."

"Said no teenager ever," I commented, glancing sideways at him.

He huffed a laugh. "Okay, I was too busy to get into *much*

trouble." Then he sighed. "In any case, I never learned anything about breaking and entering."

"It's odd, the things you live to regret." But even if we could pick the lock, we'd still need to deal with the guards. My brain skittered away from thoughts of guns. "Why set all this up out here? What were they growing that could be that important?" All the equipment and supplies had been imported, and they'd built a cage around what seemed to be the only portal here. None of that made sense unless the end product was worth far more than the initial cost.

"Normally, I'd say some sort of drug..." Christopher trailed off doubtfully.

"Yeah." If the stench of the plant was this bad normally, the concentrated version would be even worse. I went back to what my first thoughts had been when we'd entered the dome. "Some sort of pheromone? Like those hunters who spray doe urine around their blinds use?"

Christopher chewed on his lower lip while he thought about it. "That would make some sense, given the whole hunting theme going on out there."

"And if whatever they were attracting with it was dangerous enough, it might explain why they set up the process in a remote location." Having to get through a portal made it about as remote as possible. "Though that still doesn't explain the locked gate."

Christopher pulled the sleeping bag tighter. "Maybe whoever was here tried to quit. Or unionize."

The green lights moved around the dome panels as I thought about this. "I hope they aren't expecting us to grow the next batch. I killed a pothos plant once." From Christopher's low laugh, I could tell he understood. There was a reason the other name for it was devil's ivy. Antonia swore it was unkillable.

How long had we been gone? Antonia might be starting to get concerned. With any luck, she'd taken the snuggle-pups back to her place for the night and she wouldn't worry about me until morning. And by then...

No. I had a full schedule at work on Monday and I refused to get stuck here.

I pushed off the sleeping bag and stood up. "We have to get out of here. Let's break it down into steps."

Christopher stayed seated. "We need to get through the gate, and then we need to get past the guards, and then we need to find Fred, and then get back to the portal going to Paladin Research. So... we just need an acetylene torch and then a cloak of invisibility."

"Or..." I paced around the dome as I thought about what we had: a sleeping bag, a bunch of cardboard, dead plants, and some distillation supplies. "How about we make them open the gate *and* create a distraction at the same time? If we shove a bunch of the plants through the portal and light them on fire, most of the smoke will stay there, right? And if it smells as bad burning as it does normally..."

He slowly smiled. "They'll open the gate so they can get rid of it." Then worry crinkled his brow. "There's every chance this could all go wrong and get us killed."

We looked at each other for a long moment as we silently acknowledged the odds.

"You and I know too much for them to just let us leave," I said. "Might as well go down fighting."

26

Harvesting the dead plants was quick; finding a way to ignite the fuel almost stymied us.

"We might be able to start a fire with the space heater," Christopher said as he stowed another handful of plants in a cardboard box. "But it would be smothered going through the portal. Unless we could get it hot enough to flash over again once it got to the other side..." His face took on the distant look of a man who was too smart to throw gasoline on a fire, but would gleefully watch videos of other idiots trying it.

"Matches," I said firmly. "Someone here was a smoker." I left him to pull up more plants and went to search the domes again, more throughly this time.

My rummage through the distillery dome didn't produce matches, but I found a lighter and a jar of chili oil. If this didn't work and we were stuck here eating MREs, I'd regret wasting the condiment, but it would help produce a nice smoky fire that would be hard to put out.

Christopher's eyes lit up when I showed him my finds. "Excellent. If summer camp taught me anything, it's that a little cooking oil is the best way to cheat when building a fire with wet logs."

"It's probably also going to irritate your eyes and lungs, so don't stick around to watch it burn." Brown leaves rustled in the two boxes I carried to the front dome.

"Don't take all the fun out of this," he laughed as he walked behind me, laden with more fuel to smoke out the hall.

The two of us fashioned a narrow fire starter box, filled with plant stalks drizzled in chili oil. "I'll take this over, light it on fire, then come back." Christopher patted the sides of the box. "After that, we feed the rest through the portal until they open the gate."

"Perfect." Then the problem hit me. "How will we know when that's happened?"

"We'll keep trying to push this through." He nudged a carton that had originally held paper towels but now held a stinky mass of dead flora. "It's too big to fit in that space, so if it suddenly disappears, we know the first part of the plan worked."

Then we'd just need to get past all the guys with guns. No problem. I nodded. "Ready?"

"Let's do this." He draped the sleeping bag over my shoulders and opened the door.

Green light from the aurora waved across the sky, but a yellow glow on the horizon hinted of the coming dawn. We followed the packed snow back to the portal shimmering in an unseen breeze. Christopher picked up the narrow box and tested the lighter.

"Wait." Suddenly convinced this was a terrible idea, I grabbed his elbow. "Maybe we should..." I trailed off, because that was the problem. Wait for Mullins to realize we couldn't be used to force Fred to harm the world? Or worse, find out that we could? "Just... Be careful."

His face just inches from mine, Christopher nodded. "Back in a second." He turned and walked into the portal.

In a few seconds, the bright spot where he had been faded, and I was alone.

TIME STRETCHED. How long could it possibly take to ignite oil-soaked leaves and cardboard? Waves of green light trailed back and forth overhead, a Dali-esque metronome emphasizing my inability to accurately gauge the passage of time.

Finally, the center of the portal shimmered. A tightness in my chest eased when Christopher stepped out, landing a foot to the side of where he'd gone in. He was accompanied by a rank odor I could smell even over the boxes of plants by my side. Wiping his streaming eyes with one hand, he bent double, coughing. When he could finally draw a breath, he rasped, "You weren't kidding when you said I shouldn't inhale that chili oil smoke."

Huddled together under the sleeping bag, I could feel his chest spasm. "Did you see anything while you were there?"

"Just the guards that were there before. Fred and Xavier were gone, and I didn't see Mullins anywhere." He coughed again. "Someone had just noticed the fire when I left."

We pushed the larger box into the portal until it wouldn't move further. Then we fed branches through next to it. Noxious black smoke billowed up, evidence our fire still burned on the other side.

As we tended our unseen flames, melted snow seeped

through my shoes. Christopher radiated warmth, but my feet were going numb. "What if they don't have the keys?" Mullins had opened the gate with his own key ring when we'd come through.

"What if they just blast a fire extinguisher through the bars?" Christopher countered.

That one I could answer. "I didn't see any extinguishers when we were there, and I looked. Or at least, they weren't clearly marked. OSHA would not be pleased."

Christopher pulled the sleeping bag tighter. "People cut corners if nothing has to pass inspection." He held another plant up to the portal and let it get sucked through. "Makes you wonder what the construction is like in the rest of the buildings there."

A stinky resin coated my palm from handling the branches. "The whole project feels like something put together by that one guy who thinks he's smarter than everyone else. Except I bet there's normally a trail of people behind him fixing all his messes. I don't think those people are there now." Thinking of the Kentucky bluegrass again, I shook my head. "Nobody would be stupid enough to buy into that place once they saw it, would they?"

Christopher coughed. "You just don't want what they're selling enough to fall for the con."

The cardboard box we'd been using to monitor the space on the other side suddenly slid through.

Christopher moved to the left edge of the portal and nudged me behind him. "Ready?"

I squeezed his callused hand. "Ready."

He stepped in. Holding my breath, I leaned forward and let the portal take me.

27

We burst out into smoke, chaos, and a cacophony of cursing interspersed with deafening bursts of gunfire. Christopher yanked me forward, past a smoldering cardboard box. When the gate had opened, a mound of burning plants had fallen. Now the flames leaped taller than my head. Someone on the other side of the pile was beating at it with a jacket.

An unholy scream echoed off the walls. If Christopher hadn't maintained a firm grip on my hand, I would have fled back into the portal to our prison. Nothing human made that sound. With all the smoke filling the air, tears streamed down my cheeks. Haze obscured the grid of portals, and I was suddenly afraid we would blunder into one as we ran. The only light came from the open door at the other end of the hall.

We scrambled to the nearest wall. Even with the neck of my shirt over my nose, my throat tightened and I could feel the panic of oxygen starvation. "I can't breathe," I choked.

"Stay low!" Putting words into action, he pushed me toward the floor, dropping to his hands and knees. The sleeping bag sloughed off my shoulders as I crawled toward the light.

Down near the floor, the air was slightly better. Somewhere on the other side of the room, another animal screamed in rage. Gunfire followed and a man's inarticulate yell abruptly cut off. I crawled forward, my knees bruising on the concrete floor. When we were halfway to the door, the air cleared enough for us to scramble in a crouch.

We ran through the door. Outside, the air was sweet and clear, and two women jogged on the path in the distance. In front of us, tiny waves lapped at the shore of the lake. Christopher and I staggered around the side of the building and leaned against the wall, coughing and wheezing.

Inside the building, more animals screamed and men yelled. Outside, it might have been a perfect summer day. A paddle boat bobbed on the far side of the lake, powered by a man and a small boy. I realized I'd been unconsciously waiting for sirens, either police or fire, but there wouldn't be any. That infrastructure didn't exist here. Everybody was on their own.

Another salvo of gunfire reminded me that bullets could cut through walls. I didn't understand what we had unleashed, but we needed to get away right now.

After one last attempt to cough out the carcinogens, I stood up and tugged on Christopher's arm. "We have to go."

We moved to the path, trying to look like people out on a stroll, so we didn't draw attention. Both of us were trying to hold back fits of coughing. Christopher wiped at his eyes. "What happened back there? What were they shooting at?"

"I have no idea." I glanced over my shoulder. Smoke streamed out of the building. "But I don't think the people with guns were winning." Then I stopped. "You don't think Fred is in there somewhere, do you?"

Christopher pulled me forward. "Everyone I saw was wearing boots."

He didn't need to explain. Between the cast on one foot and Mark's purple, yellow, and red running shoe on the other, Fred's feet were unmistakable.

The constriction of my chest eased. We sped up to a brisk walk. Behind us, the gunfire grew suddenly louder. I ducked even as I turned, expecting to find someone aiming at us, but a guard was standing on the grass in front of the building, pointing his gun at the haze near the doorway.

Christopher and I froze as a man-sized lizard — like a smaller, more agile *T. rex* — emerged from the smoke. Standing on its back legs, it swiveled its head, taking in the surroundings. Green and copper scales glittered in the sun, from its streamlined head to the tip of its long tail that counterbalanced it like a kangaroo. I'd seen pictures, but the photos hadn't inspired fear like seeing them in person did.

"Oh, shit," I breathed. Something suspiciously like a giggle came from Christopher. I couldn't blame him. The hair on the back of my neck rose.

Christopher cleared his throat. "What *is* that thing?" His voice wavered, as if he was still considering hysterical laughter an option.

"It's a *T. bellator*. I think." This was like being in the back lot of a dinosaur movie, except in this case, the dinosaurs hadn't died out and they'd escaped containment.

The bellator threw back its head and screamed. Then it hopped down the steps, straight toward the man with the gun. Bullet after bullet tore into its flesh as it approached. The bellator made it within two feet of the guard before it dropped to the ground, twitching.

Out on the lake, the paddle boat drifted as the people inside stared.

Another bellator emerged from the building, screaming in defiance. This one was bigger and had gold patches on the flanks. The guard retreated toward the water even as he fired.

Christopher and I ran.

The ground sloped gently upward, which didn't help my aching lungs. A blue-black gopher dashed into a hole as we came near. Part of my brain was screaming about the bellator behind us, but another part latched onto the fact that the gopher was already messing up this perfect Kentucky bluegrass lawn.

The gunfire slowed. When I looked back, the second bellator had fallen. Smoke no longer poured from the building. Dropping to a walk, I panted, "I think things might be under control back there."

The portal to Paladin Research shimmered just beyond a parked golf cart, about fifty feet away. Christopher urged me to a faster walk. "I still don't understand what happened back there."

"I have a theory," I said, and then doubled over, coughing. "Pheromones," I choked out.

"Pheromones." With an arm around my back, Christopher kept me moving. "I don't get it. Who would want to attract those things?"

"Immo Ring likes to hunt bellators," I gasped. "Some bullshit thing about showing how manly he is." I struggled to get my breathing under control again. "He has the heads mounted in his meeting room. Posts the video on social media."

"Okay..."

"But bellators are only aggressive during breeding season. A couple days a year. Where's the fun in shooting a lizard lying around in the sun?" I stopped talking to catch my breath. "I think someone figured out how to make it breeding season whenever they want." Looking down at my shirt, I found it festooned with bits of leaves and reeking of smoke. "We're covered in the stuff."

Christopher turned to walk backward so he could keep an eye on what was happening behind us. "So when we burned those plants..."

I nodded. "A little smoke went through the portal to where the bellators live, and every male in the area came running to the fight." I coughed. "It's just a theory, but it fits." With the fire out, the pheromones drifting through the portal would drop.

Once the bellators were no longer a threat, the guards would regroup and notice we had escaped. We needed to be gone before then.

Christopher pivoted to walk face-forward again. "So much for a *little* diversion."

"Go big or go home." We'd arrived at the portal going to Paladin. Glancing back to see if anyone had noticed us yet, I saw another bellator crouched on the path near the building, eyes lidded and nose raised, sniffing the breeze. It turned its head toward me and opened its eyes. "Shit."

We'd done this so many times that it felt natural to reach out and take Christopher's hand. Our feet touched the barrier at the same time. The tingle of portal contact raced up our legs and engulfed us. Everything went black.

We emerged in the dark Paladin Research greenhouse. In the middle of the building, the moonlight shining through the glass illuminated the space more than the single unshielded bulb over the south door. My eyes adjusted enough to see the rows of portals spaced neatly along the length of the building.

At the southern end, two verdirans argued loudly, their outlines fuzzy from the combined opacity of tens of portals. I hoped one of them was Fred. Once we located him, we could go home. Or at least get out of here and go somewhere safer.

My clothes still reeked from the smoke. If the bellator tracking us understood portals, it might follow. Unlike in the building where we'd started the fire, the ground here was dirt. I leaned toward Christopher and whispered, "Did you see a shovel anywhere?" We needed to close this portal, to stop the bellator and keep the guards on the other side.

He jerked his head toward the north door. "This way."

We tiptoed through the gloom. Glancing back, I got a clearer look at the verdirans from the center aisle. Fred faced our direction; he had to have seen us. I wanted to reassure him we weren't abandoning him, but if he looked too closely, the other verdiran — and anyone else at that end of the building — would know we were there.

As we slipped out the door and onto the gravel path, my phone buzzed. That was probably Antonia checking in, her texts delayed until my phone had coverage again. Or...

Shit. I was on call at the emergency clinic tonight. If they'd been trying to call me... I wanted to stop and look at my phone, but this wasn't the time. We needed to get that portal closed before anyone — or anything — came through it. Besides, it wasn't like I knew all the xenotics answers either. They would just have to do their best.

I followed Christopher to another unlocked greenhouse. He reached inside and withdrew two heavy shovels, big enough for some serious digging. The last time we'd destroyed portals this way, we'd only had my small spade, which was light enough to carry on a hike and marketed to women — it had probably been marked up extra because of it.

We lugged the tools back and snuck inside again. Fred could close the portals just by... whatever it was he did when he was holding a piece of the central tree. Or maybe he didn't even need it — Mullins had said the verdirans could open portals on their own. Maybe they could close them as well. Christopher and I didn't have Fred's abilities, but if we could change the ground here so it didn't match the other side, the portal would cease to exist... unless something about these portals being anchors made them different from the ones we'd wiped out on our hike.

Stealthily digging trenches wasn't easy, but Christopher and I worked on either side of the portal leading to Pure Paradise. The trick was to dig close enough to the shimmering air to remove the dirt under it, but not so close that the shovel got sucked in.

If the latter happened, we could muscle the tool back out, or let go and find another shovel. The third option was to hang on, go through to the other side, and then immediately return. But that risked being on the wrong side when the portal closed, wearing apparel that drove bellators into a killing rage.

Verdiran growls and clicks reverberated against the glass panes, along with a second conversation by someone speaking English. Was Mullens over there with Fred and Xavier? Or had he not come back? If we didn't get this closed soon, the guards from the other side would come through.

As I dug, I tried to make out the English conversation happening forty feet away.

"... do you mean *they're loose*?" The speaker's voice rose. It was definitely Mullins. "That's what we station the guards there for."

Our portal snapped closed with a whiff of ozone. I let out a long breath in relief.

On the other side of the hall, the verdirans stopped talking. Christopher grabbed my arm and pulled me to the side, away from the center aisle and toward the darker north end of the building.

Mullins must have been on the phone because I could only hear his side of the conversation, even when he paused. "How many? What? How did *that* happen?" He paused. "Did anyone see? No, I don't care about *them*. I mean the residents? We need to control this before it scares the shareholders away."

The door ahead of us opened, and a man came through. Christopher and I reversed direction, creeping back toward the south end. We'd have to sneak around Mullins as he talked on the phone.

Xavier walked down the middle aisle toward us, Fred crutching along behind him. When the first verdiran saw the two of us, he stopped, the wood chunk in his hand, as if he had come to fix whatever had gone wrong and we were not what he was expecting. Fred waved, his eyes fierce.

A voice came from behind me. "Drop the shovels and put your hands up." I turned my head and saw Billy, the huge guy who had driven my car away. There was only one of him and two of us, but he had a gun in his hand.

"Shit," I muttered.

Christopher took a step away from me, rested the shovel blade on the dirt, and held onto the handle. "They might be spades, not shovels." He looked at me. "What's the difference, anyhow?"

My heart raced so loudly I could hear little else, but since he'd clearly directed the man's attention toward me for a reason, I picked up the conversation. "Spades have a flat blade and they're usually smaller, though you can buy cute little pink shovels if you want to waste a bunch of money. They usually fall apart the first time you dig with them. Shovel blades are curved more like a scoop." I lifted my shovel a few inches off the ground. Now I had all of Billy's attention. Pointing at the rounded edge, I added, "*This* is definitely a shovel."

While Billy was distracted, Christopher swung his shovel up like a baseball bat, connecting with the man's outstretched wrist. The gun arced up and clattered to the dirt. Billy dove for it, but I scooped it off the ground with the shovel and lobbed it through the nearest portal.

Then, inspired by Christopher's success, I swung again and hit Xavier's hand. Without as much force behind the blow, my swing didn't send the chunk of wood flying, but I did hurt him enough that he yowled and dropped it. When Xavier leaned down to pick it up again, Fred pushed him away with the end of one crutch, sending the other verdiran sprawling. I tossed the shovel, darted forward, and grabbed the chunk of wood. Fred's attention was elsewhere, so I shoved the wood in my back pocket.

Mullins ran up, still yelling into his phone. "They're here! Send backup to building seven."

Christopher grunted. I looked over just in time to see him grappling with the disarmed guard. They brushed against a portal, the one with the red metal strip in front of it. The air shimmered, and both men disappeared.

As the light from the portal faded, I froze. That was the portal to a forbidden destination. What had Mullins said? If we went through, the verdirans would abandon us there.

It didn't matter. I couldn't leave Christopher on his own.

Fred swung toward the portal and hopped in.

If I followed, I would have to trust that Fred wouldn't leave us.

Mullins grabbed my arm. "Hold still!"

I muscled my way forward, dragging him behind me. Stretching my free arm toward the shimmering lights, I extended my fingers...

Behind me I heard Mullins yell, "They're in delta 42! Send —"

His words cut off as the portal engulfed me.

29

This portal transition was uncomfortably long, reminding me of the first time Christopher and I had traveled together. Darkness pressed against me and I struggled not to panic.

By the time I came out on the other side, my oxygen reserves were gone. I'd half-expected to end up on the snowy mountain slope. Instead, I emerged in a humid swamp.

My exit wasn't graceful — Mullins let go when we came out, and I fell forward, landing on the lateral roots of an immense cypress-like tree that formed a plateau in the wide river around us. Mud and rocks drove into my forearms as I plowed to a stop. The sun was high overhead, but at ground level we were shaded by a dense canopy of trees. I'd ended up a few inches away from a drop into murky water. Everything smelled like rotten eggs.

In the distance, I could see other portals in a somewhat regular pattern, influenced by the growth of the trees. More anchors? We weren't on the snowy mountain, but something about this place felt similar.

When I rolled over, I found Fred and Christopher standing nearby. Xavier had come through after Mullins, and now he and Billy were picking their way across the roots. Mullins had fallen to one knee behind me. He stumbled toward the water as he regained his footing, caught his balance, and turned back to the portal, arms outstretched like a tightrope walker.

Christopher had his left hand shoved in his pocket, but reached down with the right to help me up. "You okay?"

I nodded, but he was slow to release my hand when I stood. When I looked over at Fred, his leg cast was soaking up water from the mud around his toes. He stared at Xavier, looked at our surroundings, and growled.

Keeping my movements hidden from the other group, I passed Fred the portal controller. With a minute tilt of his head, he dropped the wood into his pocket.

Our portal closed.

I looked up at Fred's face. When in doubt, confuse your enemy. Fred was definitely on our team. But there also seemed more to the gesture. Fred was... upset? Angry that we were here? I remembered his reaction to my drawing of the regular grid of portals. This place was a dangerous secret as well.

Mullins froze in disbelief. "What...?" His face paled. Turning to Xavier, he pointed to the ground with his free hand. "Bring it back. Now!"

Xavier stared off into the distance while Mullins yelled orders at him.

I kept my voice low. "Did you hurt your shoulder again?"

Christopher massaged his shoulder. "Still in the socket. No need to put me down yet."

I blew out a breath. "That was quite the swing back there."

"Thanks. One season of Little League went a long way."
He raised his brows. "You going out for professional jai alai?
That was a nice scoop and toss."

"Lacrosse," I corrected. "Varsity for two years in high
school."

"Impressive."

"There was only one team, and it got me out of regular
P.E."

Something big roiled the water. I shuffled a little closer
to the tree trunk, suddenly nervous about what was hiding
in the murk. With the added humidity, the odor of my shirt
was hard to ignore. I could only hope there weren't any
bellators anywhere around here.

A large pink bird squawked and flew from a nearby tree,
skimming over the water before plucking out a fish and
rising again. "I don't suppose you've been here before."
Christopher had led expeditions through portals as part of
the DPAS in Florida. Maybe he would know the dangers to
watch out for here.

"No, sorry."

Fred hissed to get our attention and gestured to the river
where a nutria swam. A snake erupted from the tea-colored
water, wrapped around the rodent's body, and dragged it
under. Except... That hadn't been a snake. I swallowed.
"Grabber?" We'd run into a pond of the possibly fungal
predators during our hike, but the grabber's tendrils hadn't
moved as independently as whatever had attacked this
animal.

Next to me, Christopher hummed his disagreement.
"Maybe some animal with tentacles?"

Fred tapped him on the arm and pointed to a columnar
tree fifty feet away, one with a trunk that went straight down
into the water.

I sidled away from the river. "Is he really saying those are tree tentacles?"

"I think so." Christopher sounded fascinated by the knowledge. I just wanted to go back home.

The water churned where the nutria had disappeared, and the rodent bobbed back up to the surface, a two-foot section of chewed off tentacle dangling from its mouth. It climbed up on the roots of a tree similar to the one where we stood, then held the still twitching morsel and nibbled daintily.

Christopher cleared his throat. "At least it's not a snake."

Out of the corner of my eye, I saw Xavier reach out and push Mullins out of his way. Then he said something to Fred.

Mullins moved back in front of Xavier. "Listen to me! You need to get us *back* to *earth*. Understand? *Back* to *earth!*" Xavier didn't acknowledge him.

I couldn't understand why Fred hadn't created a portal to get us out of here. He and Xavier seemed to expect something would happen.

An image of Antonia waiting for me to come home made my chest tight. I wanted to be safe in my own house, with my mother-in-law on the other side of the yard and my animals curled up on my bed. Everything would be fine if I could just go home.

Mullins's continual yelling broke into my thoughts. I cut him off mid-sentence. "Give it a rest." I waved my hand at the sky. "His remote control is back in building seven." That was a lie, but I didn't want to make Fred a target.

A look of confusion went over Mullins's face, and then his fists clenched. "He left... No. He wouldn't do that. The navigators don't travel without a piece of the central tree." Mullins stared at Xavier, taking in the hand the verdiran cradled against his chest. "You don't understand." His voice was quick, on the edge of panic. "We need to get back before any other verdirans arrive. If they get here first, that's it. We're not supposed to be here. Neither of *them* will risk being shunned to get us out."

Something in the way he spoke told me he *knew* that, as if it had come up before. The pieces fell into place. "So we'll just be like the other employees who disappeared." I looked at Christopher. "What was your friend's name?"

"Nam Nguyen."

"No." Mullins shook his head. "The explorers know the risks when they take the job. They get paid extra for trips through the red portals. We didn't mean to come here. This is different."

It was only different because Mullins was the one getting left behind. "So what happened to the employees who disappeared?"

"There were accidents. Some of the anchors the navigator created weren't viable in the long term. There were unavoidable losses along the way."

My neck was so tense I'd have a headache soon. "So why didn't you have him create a new portal to get them back?"

"We weren't supposed to be sending anyone through them, so we couldn't exactly complain if they vanished." He shook his head and gave me a look as if I was a particularly stupid child. "You don't understand. We *had* to study these places. There's no other way to find out what the verdirans know."

Except they hadn't figured anything out that I hadn't learned in a few days with Fred staying at my house. This man had threatened my entire state, and for what? A few hundred acres of pretty grass and the ability to hunt large prey whenever the investors wanted?

Christopher's voice was flat. "Does your boss know it's all a sham, or is that going to be a surprise to him when he tries to move to your new paradise?"

"Immo? He knows there have been setbacks. With a moonshot like this, it's to be expected. Immo's a big picture guy. Sometimes the details take a while to get worked out."

I couldn't help myself. "He thinks he's a genius because he pays people to tell him how smart he is." If anyone had ever had the guts to tell Immo Ring his ideas were stupid, the Chevalier Foundation wouldn't have wiped out all the xenoflora so they could plant one cultivar of grass. Even *I* knew that wouldn't work, and I was a veterinarian, not a botanist. Everyone involved with the program must have known it was a bad idea.

"It's attitudes like yours that halt progress. We just need a little more time to work out the rest of the technical challenges..."

He trailed off as another portal flowed into being on our island of roots. Fred stood up straighter.

Mullins paled.

Three verdiran women stepped out. They were stooped and wrinkled with age, but they moved easily enough over the uneven roots. The woman in the front saw the humans and drew back. Fred listened to her harsh exclamation and inclined his head toward Xavier.

Danger. Secret. Unless I missed my guess, these were the people Fred had been warning me about.

The shortest woman walked to the spot where our portal had been before Fred had closed it. With green fingers rippling in the air, she traced the outline. Another new bit of information: the verdirans could sense closed portals. When I glanced at Fred, he was watching Xavier.

The woman let her hands fall, walked across the roots to Xavier, and cuffed his head.

Xavier didn't raise a hand to defend himself, but he spoke, the words rushing from him as if he were pleading for her to understand. Even without translating his speech, I could tell he was arguing the same case he'd made to Fred at my house about finding the lost verdirans. Despite getting caught in this place, Xavier remained committed to his cause.

The oldest verdiran raised a hand gnarled by arthritis, and Xavier's words stumbled to a halt. The ancient woman slowly enunciated a phrase. Xavier exhaled, his breath turning into a moan.

The tallest woman repeated the phrase, giving each syllable a gravitas I didn't hear in their normal speech.

Finally, the verdiran who had hit Xavier repeated the syllables. When she was done, her eyes unfocused. She turned, as if Xavier no longer stood there. Without acknowledging him further, she moved back to the verdirans she had come with.

Xavier's head slumped forward. His skin took on a grey tinge.

Back at Paladin, Mullins had said the verdirans would shun Xavier if they found out he had allowed humans to come to this place. I still wasn't sure exactly what that meant in practice, but from Xavier's response, it was life-altering.

The old verdirans looked at Fred, completely ignoring Christopher and me. Once again, humans were creatures that wouldn't be named. Fred gestured for us to move forward, toward the older verdirans and their portal. I hoped it led back to earth.

The ancient woman growled, holding up her palms to stop our progress.

Fred moved behind Christopher and me. He slapped one hand down on the other palm in a negation that startled a flock of yellow birds from a nearby tree.

The three elderly verdirans regarded him silently, then one after another, they tapped their fingertips on their palms, united in their *yes*. Fred remained firm in his negation. He wasn't leaving without us.

I was so busy watching Fred argue that I almost missed Mullins sneaking toward the portal, with Billy close behind. Clearly, they thought sneaking to an unknown destination was better than relying on Fred — or Xavier — to get us out of here.

My gut said Mullins was wrong. But seeing Xavier slumped on the roots, I worried. These were Fred's people. What were Christopher and I to him? Friends? We might be at some point, but we'd only known each other for a few days. Surely that couldn't be worth losing his entire culture. Maybe Mullins was making the smart move.

The only thing I knew for certain was that Mullins wouldn't send help if he got away.

Fred was still arguing when Mullins reached the portal. The man's look of triumph nearly made me interrupt, to point out what was happening, but I kept quiet. Destroying Mullins's chances wouldn't improve my own.

He touched the portal. A spark flashed and he yanked his hand back. "What the hell?" Billy threw his shoulder against the same spot as if he were breaking down a door. With a crackle of electricity, he was knocked backward.

Mullins shook out his fingertips. Panic touched his voice. "This isn't possible."

The oldest verdiran facing Fred spoke, the tones of her growls and clicks familiar now that I'd heard them three times before.

"Wait!" I waved my hands. "You can't do this. It's not *his* fault we're here."

But the woman beside her didn't even look at me. She held her chin up and repeated the phrase. Next to me, Fred shuddered as the third woman recited the words.

This time I saw the move in triplicate, as all three of the old verdirans looked past him, no longer seeing Fred.

"No," I breathed.

Fred stood still as granite.

The old verdirans turned and walked to their portal. It admitted them without issue and closed in their wake.

Everyone stood frozen as the tang of ozone dissipated. Water rippled as the river flowed, the only proof that time hadn't stopped. My helplessness was reflected in Christopher's eyes. Fred didn't seem to notice when I put my hand on his shoulder, so I let my arm drop.

Mullins threw out his hands and snarled at us. "You've ruined *everything*! Now we're *stuck* here."

Fred's movements were stiff as he pulled the portal remote from his pocket. Mullins saw the movement and his shoulders relaxed. "Oh, thank god."

Without a sound or a sideways glance, Xavier stood and stumbled into the water. Fred shoved the wood back in his pocket, dropped his crutches, and grabbed the other verdiran by the shoulders, hauling his struggling form back onto dry land. Xavier keened.

"Grab that central tree!" Mullins yelled to Billy.

If Mullins got hold of that piece of wood, he would have all the leverage he needed. Christopher's reactions were faster than mine — he intercepted Billy. That left me to keep Mullins at bay.

The Chevalier Foundation's technical director had four inches and at least sixty pounds on me. Meanwhile, I had knowledge of where all the major muscle groups were. He looked at me, shook his head like he couldn't believe I'd bother challenging him, and easily blocked the kick I aimed at his knee. His motion looked automatic, as if he practiced hand to hand combat. "Fuckaduck," I whispered to myself.

I stood my ground as much as I could on the muddy roots, thinking about how to evade a punch. But he bent down, grabbed me around the waist, and in one smooth motion, flipped me in an arc toward the murky water.

30

A s I flew through the air, time slowed. I saw Christopher's head turn as he tracked my movements. He took half a step in my direction. Fred — Xavier struggling in his arms — met my eyes.

Then I hit the chilly water. Foul tasting fluid flooded my mouth. I propelled myself up to the surface and floundered back toward the platform. Kicking required a huge effort, my sodden jeans and shoes hampering every movement. By luck, my flailing arm hit a solid root. I clutched it, but just as I was pulling myself up, something wrapped around my ankle and yanked me down.

Water closed over my head mid-breath. The roots were slick with mud, and I lost my first handhold and scrabbled wildly until I found another. Still underwater, I reached down to pull at the band around my ankle, trying to sink my nails into its soft flesh. Slime oozed over my fingers. Another tentacle brushed against my forearm. Struggling to maneuver in jeans, I used my other foot to kick off my shoe. That let me slip from its grasp, and I broke the surface, choking and coughing. I heard Christopher yell my name.

Before I could get out of the water, the tentacle had wrapped around my angle again. I couldn't pull away — this thing was stronger than I was.

But the tiny nutria had defeated it. Fred had made sure we'd seen that.

Taking a lungful of air, I forced myself to let go of my handhold and dove down into the murky water.

Grabbing the tentacle in both hands, I raised it to my face and bit down. Acidic and salty fluid filled my mouth, making my stomach heave. I ruthlessly overrode that instinct — if I vomited now, I'd drown. Tearing off the piece with my teeth, I spat it out and bit through the rest. When it went limp, I dropped the tentacle and kicked up to the surface. This time, I hauled myself halfway out of the water before something grabbed my other ankle and yanked.

Billy and Christopher grappled on the ground, fairly evenly matched for all that Billy had nearly twice the bulk. But as I watched, Mullins picked up a thick branch and stood over them, arm raised, waiting for a clear shot at Christopher's head. In my mind, I saw the branch come down and fracture Christopher's skull, saw this good and kind man lying discarded, eyes open, blood running into the water. "No!" My rage spilled from my mouth. I wouldn't let that happen.

The thing in the water pulled me inexorably down, and my arms trembled with the effort of staying where I was. Screw it. If I was going to drown and be eaten by some tentacled beast, I'd take Mullins with me.

With the last of my energy, I hauled myself up, abandoned my grip on the roots, and wrapped my arms around Mullins's calves. When the tentacles pulled me down, I dragged Mullins into the water with me. He landed with an enormous splash. Together, we were yanked down to the river bottom, where we thumped into a floor of decaying vegetation and bones.

More prepared this time, I didn't end up with a lungful of water. After I released Mullins's legs, I doubled over and chewed at another tentacle, gagging at the bitter salt. We were stirring up so much muck with our struggling, I couldn't see anything, but Mullins's terrified frenzy roiled the water nearby. A storm of bubbles rose as he screamed.

With one last bite of salty flesh, I freed myself. Then I climbed arm over arm up Mullins's body and pushed off his shoulders. As I kicked to move through the water, my feet hit his forehead. I'd lost all sense of direction, but the bubbles guided me up. The surface suddenly appeared in front of me.

Gulping air, I splashed to the platform, forcing my heavy legs to propel me forward. I grabbed the roots once again and tried to pull myself out of the water, but my arms failed. Another tentacle wrapped around my waist, pulling me back. Splinters knifed into my flesh as my fingers slid along the roots.

I wasn't going to make it out.

For just an instant, I pictured myself letting go. Death had never been my greatest fear. Death could be a welcome release. And this would be quick, a few minutes of pain and then endless peace. Murky water rose above my nostrils as I sank. Then I glimpsed Christopher and Fred, still struggling with their opponents.

No. Letting go now would be cowardice — I refused to be that selfish. I tilted my head back and drew an aching breath, willing my fingers to hang on just a little longer.

Through a swirl of sediment, I saw Fred bow his head. Sorrow and pain flashed over his features. When he lifted his face again, he released Xavier and lunged forward to grab my arm. Fred hauled me out of the river and stomped his cast on the tentacle. The pressure around my stomach abated as the tendril slithered back into the water.

I collapsed on the solid roots, exhausted and breathless. With the last of my strength, I shoved myself farther from the water's edge. Fred slipped on the muddy roots and landed heavily, but before I could check if he was hurt, Xavier screamed in anguish. I looked over just in time to witness him plunge into the water. A tentacle rose out of the river and whipped around his neck. Bubbles rose as the tree pulled him under.

The surface of the river quieted.

With a low moan, Fred collapsed next to me, staring at the water where Xavier had disappeared.

Billy backed warily away from Christopher, hands up, as if he'd just realized Mullins was gone. Both of them were panting and covered in cuts and bruises.

I coughed and vomited a slurry of swamp water and tentacle blood. Pollen drifted down, swirling patterns onto the surface of the slowly flowing river. Of Xavier and Kirk Mullins, there was no sign. My ankle burned. My shoulder felt like it was close to being ripped out of the socket. I could almost hear the bacteria teeming in my lungs from the fetid soup I'd inhaled. But I was still alive.

Around us, the entire swamp slept. Occasional glimmers from distant portals added an otherworldly air. "Christopher?" I coughed. "Are you okay?" My dripping clothes weighed me down.

"Just fine," he croaked. From the way he sounded, he'd either taken a blow to the throat, or the guard had tried to choke him. "You?"

"I'm good." My first two attempts to rise failed, but on the third try, I pushed myself onto my hands and knees. Fred didn't move. At some point, his cast had gone into the water up to mid-shin; it was a soggy mess. He started when I put a hand on his shoulder, the misery on his face transcending our communication differences. I settled next to him and looked out at the water, unwilling to have it at my back. "Thank you," I breathed. We still didn't have a sign for that yet.

He had let Xavier die to save me.

Another huge pink bird glided down from the top of the tentacle tree. Everything was so alien, but also somehow familiar. My cough turned into another bout of vomiting, which didn't make the taste in my mouth any worse. Whatever those tentacles were made of, it wasn't something I ever wanted to chew on again.

Holding Fred's crutches, Christopher limped across the roots. I didn't know if he meant to remind Fred we were still there and needed his help to get back home, or if he was just being helpful. Either way, Fred straightened his shoulders and struggled to his feet. He turned in a full circle to look at the surroundings, as if trying to preserve this moment in his memories. After that, he maneuvered closer to the spot Xavier had created the original portal.

Christopher offered me his good arm and I struggled to my feet.

Eyes closed, Fred dropped his chin to his chest. Slowly, light spread from a pinpoint at eye level, going up and down until it formed a vertical line. Then it widened. Fred nodded us through.

"Wait!" In a panicked rush, Billy came forward. "Don't leave me here."

We wouldn't do that, I wanted to say. But I couldn't claim some moral high ground here. A few minutes before, I'd intentionally fed Kirk Mullins to the beast under the water.

No matter what the justification, I'd killed a man today. So I just waited for Billy to enter, and then Christopher supported me as we followed him through.

When we came out, we weren't at Paladin Research. Everything was dark, but the smell of dirt and asphalt suggested we were out on one of the county roads. My eyes adjusted, and I wasn't surprised to find we were at the corner where I'd dropped Christopher and Fred off earlier in the evening.

Christopher and I staggered to the side of the portal, staring at it, and I knew we both had the same fear, that Fred would wade out into the water like Xavier. Surely he would be coming here with us. But I should have made him go through before me... though the thought of being the last person on yet another planet terrified me.

The center of the portal brightened. Fred stepped out, nearly collapsing as one crutch skidded away. I scooted sideways and put an arm around him to take his weight. Then I doubled over to cough and we both hit the ground. So much for supporting Fred.

Behind us, the portal winked out, leaving only a whiff of ozone behind.

When I'd caught my breath and Fred and I had helped each other up, I heard Christopher and Billy speaking in low voices.

"... signed an NDA," the guard said. "They take those things seriously."

"At least some of what they're doing there is illegal, and NDAs won't apply," Christopher responded. "DPAS can protect you if you talk to them."

"You don't know these people. I'm out." Billy's footsteps receded.

Christopher made a low grunt of frustration. Then he

came to stand by us. When he put a hand on my sopping shoulder, he moved closer, the heat coming from his body welcome in the chilly night. "We need to get you some dry clothes. Any idea where your car is?"

"No." My voice came out as a rasp. "They drove it somewhere when they grabbed me." I dug my phone out of my pocket, but wasn't surprised when it didn't light up. "Shit." I really should have paid for the waterproof case. "Is your phone still working?" Christopher hadn't gone swimming with his. He probably had a waterproof case anyhow.

"I ditched it in a greenhouse at Paladin before we surrendered ourselves, so anyone looking for us would have a place to start asking questions if we didn't come back."

That had been a great idea, showing foresight and resourcefulness. It also meant we were stuck in the middle of nowhere with no ride. We both looked at the dark county roads. No cars had driven past since we'd arrived.

It was going to be a long walk home.

31

In the end, Christopher jogged the mile to the nearest farmhouse so he could call Antonia, the only person either of us knew with a publicly listed phone number.

Fred and I sat together in the dirt, waiting for Christopher to return. My ankle burned in a way that made me pretty sure the tentacle had tried to digest me. Since it was too dark to examine the skin, I tried to pretend it was just a little abrasion.

Without my phone, Fred and I couldn't communicate through the app, but his dejected posture told me everything. Plus, he seemed surprised every time I spoke or acknowledged him in any way. As if he thought at some point I would begin looking past him and pretend he didn't exist.

When Antonia arrived with her elderly Buick, she had Christopher in the passenger seat. "I was so worried about you," she said, as she bundled both Fred and me in blankets, and then bustled us into the car. "Let's get you warmed up first, and then you can tell me all about it." She sucked in her breath when she saw my ankle. "Hospital first."

Now that I could see the damage, my leg *really* hurt. A thick band of blisters encircled my ankle, except in areas where the skin had already sloughed. The whole thing was covered in a combination of blood and some gelatinous ooze — I decided not to touch it with my bare fingers. Folding my hands in my lap, I looked out the window. "Or we could go to the vet clinic and I'll clean it up there."

"Hospital," she said firmly. "For once, someone else can take care of you."

WITH FRIENDS who could easily patch up wounds and read x-rays, I'd gotten in the habit of avoiding human hospitals, so I'd forgotten how different things could be with an advocate. Between Antonia organizing the nursing staff, and Christopher borrowing her phone to call half of the DPAS, things happened quickly. Or maybe it was just that the emergency room wasn't busy.

They cut off what was left of Fred's cast, x-rayed his leg again, then set him up in a brace. In the meantime, my ankle got cleaned up and bandaged, and then the doctor listened to my lungs and it was my turn to go off to radiology.

First, though, I had to prove I wasn't pregnant. My protests that it was physically impossible were waved away. When I asked if they just planned to ignore my lungs if I *was* pregnant, Antonia thrust the cup at me with narrowed eyes, and then turned and distracted the doctor. On the other side of the room, Christopher carefully studied a flaw in the paint near Fred's bed. I was too tired to be stubborn, so I limped off in my hospital gown to pee in the cup. "Sure, parthenogenesis could happen," I grumbled. "Might as well test *everyone*."

I was still waiting for the results when Christopher came back and handed me a box containing a phone. "That's the only kind they had in the gift shop," he said, holding up an identical model. We sat side by side and downloaded the translation app. "I'm worried about Fred," he admitted.

"Me, too. The soccer videos were a bust?"

"It's like he's checked out completely."

I glanced over at the other corner. Antonia sat next to Fred, one hand on his shoulder. He stared listlessly at her phone. From the sound of it, they were watching funny pet videos. "He let his friend die so he could rescue me."

"You know that wasn't your fault, right?"

Intellectually, I did. "Still feels like it." The download circle rotated on the screen. I tried to remember how to get my contacts list back. In the grand scheme of things, it was a tiny problem, but it felt like an insurmountable hurdle, one worthy of staying in bed for the next week. Keeping my voice level, I added, "I killed Mullins."

"Bullshit. It was either him or you. No jury would convict you."

"Nobody has jurisdiction." Except maybe the verdirans. And they could shun me all they wanted. "It still happened."

"He slipped." Christopher shook his head when I opened my mouth to protest. "That's what my DPAS report will say." He leaned forward, and his voice was barely audible. "You do *not* want to be the person Immo Ring blames for his death."

He had a point. The billionaire took credit for all successes and publicly blamed others for his failures. Pure

Paradise was about to become his biggest failure yet. "We weren't the only ones there."

Christopher relaxed in his chair. "Billy has his own reasons for keeping his mouth shut. I'm pretty sure he's getting a new ID right about now."

"What? He has my car!" I stood up, ready to go off to start the search in stupid hospital socks and a drafty gown, but the sudden movement made me start coughing again. I slumped back into the chair.

Christopher sounded like he was trying not to laugh. "Nessa. Billy's not stupid enough to drive around in a stolen car. I'm sure it's just parked in a lot somewhere. We'll find it."

"Sure. If nobody else steals it first. I never should have let your cousin clean it. Nobody would have dared take it then."

He cleared his throat. "They might have torched it just to improve the environment." Then he reached over and picked up my phone.

"What are you doing? I got the app to load."

"Just checking something."

Before I could respond, the nurse came to tell me the good news — I hadn't miraculously conceived a baby and I could go get my chest x-rayed.

32

Two hours later, we were all finally back at my house. Christopher and I sat on the couch. Antonia had stashed the hat she'd been knitting for Fred and gone back to her cottage to get some sleep before organizing a search for my car. Soon, everyone in town older than seventy would be out looking. But only after it got light outside. None of Antonia's friends liked to drive in the dark.

Fred sat inert on the ugly recliner, staring off into space. The cats had picked up on his mood, or else they were attracted by his unmoving state — either way, Twitter and Dumbo were curled up in his lap, and the snuggle-pups were snoring on his chest.

Christopher stopped typing on his laptop and closed the lid. As if she'd been waiting for him to finish working, Taco landed on his shoulder, carrying one of the spoons she'd stolen and stashed elsewhere in the house. I'd be eating my cereal with a fork in the morning unless I raided Antonia's kitchen.

I eyed him. "Do you still have a job?"

"I'll know in the morning. I didn't mention Mullins was on the phone with Director Noonan — that leaves me one more piece to play if they make too much noise about firing me. But the info about anchors and what we saw in Pure Paradise is out there. I copied enough people on the email that it will be hard to bury."

I noticed he hadn't said it would be impossible. "At least with Xavier... gone, we don't need to worry about more anchors being changed."

"Maybe." Christopher accepted the spoon from Taco. "Thank you." When she flew off, he passed it to me. "But Xavier's goal was to reach the missing people. He might not have been the only one trying. We're going to need to work with the verdirans to make sure that doesn't happen."

He meant DPAS needed to work with the verdiran embassy, but how much cooperation would there be when neither group saw the others as people?

Speaking of which... I typed two words into the new phone, then crossed the room and crouched next to the recliner. "Hey," I said, to get Fred's attention. Dumbo raised her head, yawned, and settled again. Concentrating, I slowly sounded out the glottal stops, with a voiced inhale between two clicks. His name.

It wasn't correct. It wasn't even as good as Christopher's effort despite thirty minutes of tutoring while Fred was in radiology. But it was close enough to make Fred turn his head and look at me for the first time since we'd come home.

I handed him the phone so he could see what I'd written. "*Thank you.*"

For a moment, I thought he was going to go back to staring into the distance. Then he reached up to caress one snuggle-pup and said his name slowly. I'd missed at least one grunt and possibly some tone he was making in his nasal cavity.

He blinked at my next attempt and repeated the sounds.

"Ugh." I tried again. Across the room, Christopher snorted. "Do verdirans have a neck sac like an ostrich? I can't make that noise." I got through half of it and Fred hissed and clapped a hand over his eyes.

Had I finally managed to offend him? There would be a certain sad irony to that, given that he'd been ostracized by his own people for allowing me to see some sacred place and leave again.

Then he dropped his hand, and I saw the wrinkle in his brow, faint but present. He shook his head.

I drew in a breath to try again. Blew it out. "Fred."

This time, he nodded.

Over on the couch, Christopher muttered, "Thank you."

"Someday, we may even find out what his name means." A yawn obliterated the end of my words.

Christopher stood and stowed his laptop under one arm. "You're off tomorrow... today, right? I'll come over later with the truck and we can join the search for your car."

"You don't have to..." I trailed off and tried again. "Thank you."

His face relaxed into a smile. Then he waved to Fred. "See you in the morning."

As I closed the door behind him, Taco landed on my shoulder with another spoon. I scratched her forehead. "For me? Thank you."

In the space of a few days, everything had changed. Fred had lost his entire community and a friend. I'd killed a man. Somehow, we would both have to come to grips with that.

But we'd also found the reason the portal instability had worsened, and we'd started fixing the problem. Plus, I'd gained a roommate and two snuggle-pups. And Christopher.

Sprawled on my couch, I looked through my new phone, trying to figure out what he had been doing to it at the hospital. There weren't any unexpected apps, and the camera roll was empty. Then I realized my contacts list was no longer blank.

"I figured out what you did," I texted.

Less than thirty seconds later, my phone buzzed. *"Just in case you want to call."*

I smiled and sent him a series of emojis: circus tent, fire engine, tornado, and safety vest. A fairly comprehensive description of my life lately. If that didn't scare the man off, nothing would.

Across the room, Dumbo snored loudly from her spot atop Fred. When the first light of dawn hit the windows, I heard the exultant bugles of the fire lizards in their nest about the front door as their new hatchling emerged into the world.

READY FOR MORE XENOTICS ADVENTURES WITH *Nessa? Join my free newsletter to receive stories and updates on the release schedule for the next volume in The Portal Storms!*

https://tmbaumgartner.com/subscribe/

ACKNOWLEDGMENTS

As always, I need to thank my critique partners, both for pointing out problems in the manuscript and also for providing general support and encouragement. Writing would be a very lonely business indeed, if I didn't have this community.

Special thanks this time around to my sister Johanna (a structural engineer), who walked me through the different types of bridges when I asked her about how to set up the metaphor. If I got it wrong, it's not her fault.

Once again, my brother Eric (originally an electrical engineer — you might have noticed a theme) checked this manuscript for typos and other problems. I feel obligated to note he pointed out that a person *can* be tried in American courts for the murder of a US citizen that occurred outside the country (in certain circumstances), but I left Nessa's comment about jurisdiction in place because *she* didn't know that. But if there any other problems, they're definitely Eric's fault.

ABOUT THE AUTHOR

T. M. Baumgartner is a speculative fiction writer who has difficulty following directions. This probably explains why the IRS recalculates her tax refund after she files it every year. At various times she has been a veterinarian, Unix system administrator, software developer, and after-hours book-shelver in a medical library.

Theresa currently lives in Northern California in a house with too many animals. She knits hats for garden gnomes and fails to grow tomatoes despite living in the perfect climate.

She also writes cozy mysteries under the pen name Tess Baytree.

Want updates about new releases? Silly dog anecdotes? Free stories? Join the newsletter mailing list! Go to https://tmbaumgartner.com/subscribe/ or point your phone's camera at the QR code above.

The marketing department here at Speculative Turtle Press is great at tail wagging, but a little challenged by tasks that require thumbs.

If you enjoyed this book and would like to help other

readers find it, please tell your friends and consider leaving a review at your favorite site.

ALSO BY T.M. BAUMGARTNER

As T.M. Baumgartner:

Shift Happens

The Chaos Job (Jackpot Drift #1)

The Chaos Connection (Jackpot Drift #2)

The Chaos Nexus (Jackpot Drift #3)

Dragon Freehold

All Gremlins Great & Small (The Portal Storms novella)

All Rocs Wise & Wonderful (The Portal Storms #1)

As Tess Baytree:

Death Walks a Dog

Death Tracks the Scent

Death Smells a Rose

Death Trims the Tree